IN THE SHADOW

of PHARAOH

DonnaRae Menard

This book is a work of fiction. All persons, details and events are products of the author's imagination or embellished facts.

Certain geographical locations in which this novel is set are real; however, liberties have been taken by the author regarding specific places within the setting.

Library of Congress Cataloging-in-Publication Data

In the Shadow of Pharaoh/Menard, D.

Title ID # 4847050
ISBN 10 # 1500131539
ISBN 13 #978-1500131531

DoRaMe Enterprises
PO Box 1478
Conway, NH 03818-1478

Though every effort is made to correct errors of spelling, grammar, and punctuation periodically mistakes sneak through. I accept full responsibility for these errors and apologize for them. If you find an error or inconsistency that should be addressed feel free to contact me with your findings. I hope you enjoy reading this book as much as I enjoyed writing it.

DEDICATION

To Therese Jean Fortin Menard (my mother)

and

Blanche Irene Menard (my grandmother)

women who allowed me to go as far as I could run

ACKNOWLEDGMENTS

Thank you to everyone who read, criticized,

corrected and supported me.

Thank you to the Jackson Women Writers

Group who always laughed and opened every door.

Thank you to Joanne Clarey, author and Kathy

Bahr, author-to-be.

Thank you to Tiffany R. Kendall, Copy Editor

who drilled me regarding semi-colons.

Thank you to LaRee Bryant, Copy Editor.

Marge Hakey, Lead Beta Girl

Cover Art by Christopher Jacovou , Social City

Consulting.

INTRODUCTION

Born into a poverty-stricken family in the slums of ancient Egypt, sold into slavery to work as a servant in Pharaoh's Palace, Ankh fights for survival for herself and the boy-child secretly sired by the Pharaoh's only male heir–a child that might one day lay claim to Hokakhty's throne.

2400 BC, Ancient Egypt

CHAPTER 1

With the loving care her mother showed to her, little Ankh

selected a pebble from the pile then offered it to her precious

doll. The ever-unmerciful Egyptian sun beat down upon her

unnoticed. B'na, her aunt, had sat her there, telling her not to

wander. Beyond the low doorway, within their small single

room home, Ankh could hear her mother's cry of pain. The old

women who sat outside quieted their chatter for a brief second

as they, too, listened. When the cry of a newborn did not

sound, they continued their gossip.

   At her mother's cry, Ankh hugged the doll to her naked

chest. Made of rag and stick it was envied by many, for few

other children possessed a toy. Ankh never left her beloved

baby behind because thieves roamed the encampments at nights. Woe that her beloved doll be taken.

At last, a wail of anger and fear brought the old women to their feet. Ankh crept closer. She wanted her mother; she was afraid. Smeared with blood, the midwife, tall and barrel-shaped, pushed through the door. She held out a scraggly, wrinkled being. He wailed loudly. The old women cheered. Aunt B'na struggled through the women. Kneeling next to Ankh, she whispered, "Just a few more minutes, Pretty One. I will come to you soon. You will be first to see your new brother."

Aunt B'na pulled away, her brief hug leaving Ankh staggering without the woman's support. The elders had finally moved away. Here in the poor quarters, there was always much to do. The wait for a birth had passed; with a blessing from the gods, this boy-child might possibly live. Ankh sat in the sun alone. When Aunt B'na finally returned, she found Ankh asleep, curled in a sliver of shade against the mud wall. Coaxing the child to wakefulness, B'na led the way to Mother's bedside. Without hesitation, Ankh reached for the security of her mother.

"No, no, do not touch him." Aunt B'na pulled the scrawny three-year-old back. "He is too small for you to play with." To Ankh's mother, B'na said, "Sister, you know this child is old enough to work. Why is she still here? She takes food your son will need, but gives nothing to the pot."

"She is my baby." The birth had been difficult. Strain and weariness softened Mother's voice. Three times she had birthed a son; three times a dead child had left her womb. "Little one, breathe, live. She had prayed with this birth. "I am too old to give you a brother."

B'na sighed, rolling her eyes to the heavens. Tenderly, she touched her sister's forehead.

"I have left food for your husband's evening meal. This broth is for you; do not feed it to the girl. Already darkness is falling and the workers return. Rest."

After she was gone, Ankh stood watching the child suckling at her mother's breast. Her great brown eyes peered into the dim light. *Why is he so honored?* She wondered. *He is so ugly.*

Her mother drew the little girl close. She had lost so many children. Ankh and her eight-year-old sister, Tusat, were all that remained. Tears gathered in her eyes as she shared the broth with her child, despite her sister's admonitions. Soon, Ankh, too, would have to leave childhood behind.

Here, the mud houses of the freemen were built along the edge of the great city. The one- or two-roomed abodes were stacked one upon the other to create ridges of neighborhoods. They were not slaves, but they were no better. A man who owned slaves made sure his property was fed and protected from the elements. Here, man and woman toiled from the hour before dawn until long after darkness and many often went to bed hungry. If they were lucky, or strong enough, they worked for Pharaoh, building the great temples and palaces his rule demanded. Both Ankh's father and her older sister were so honored. Father carved the legend of Pharaoh into the stone, while Tusat, a water carrier, toted the heavy skin water bag from worker to worker while they labored in the hot sun. Sometimes, as she passed her father, he would smile at her. It was her only reward.

Any day Father did not work for Pharaoh's cause, he would leave early to go to the great marketplace located deep within the city. There, if his luck still held, a merchant would give him work for the day.

On the first market day following the birth of his son, Father did not rise before the sun, nor did he leave before all woke. Early morning found Ankh playing with her doll in the open corridor between the houses again. People bustled by. When a shadow crossed the child and held, she looked up from her chattering play.

Father smiled at her. Tusat beamed broadly at Ankh as she held father's hand tightly.

"We are going to the market." The larger girl giggled. The only garment she owned, a worn tunic, was still damp from rinsing. Ankh hugged her doll tightly.

"Leave the doll, child." A slight frown was Father's only sign of displeasure at the sight of the toy. Ankh carefully placed her precious one inside the doorway, then took father's hand and skipped away. Mother stepped out into the sun; tears stained her cheeks. Cradling the doll to her breast, she took it to hide away. It was the only witness to the pain her last glimpse of her daughters caused her.

Skirting the small marketplace in their quarter, the three hurried along the crowded thoroughfare. Ankh and Tusat chattered excitedly. They had been allowed to sleep alone on the roof since there had been many visitors to view the baby. Now they were going to the great marketplace. Father listened in silence, thinking of the terse conversations that had come between man and wife. The girls had not heard their mother weep in the night.

As the streets widened, the populace changed, becoming rude and sour-faced. One person shoved another out of the way. That person fell into Ankh, pulling her out of Father's grasp. Father did not say a word, but snatched her up on his shoulders. She looked in amazement about her at the brightly colored robes and fancy black wigs. Fleas and lice were a common problem. A shaved head offered comfort. Ankh ran her fingers over Father's bald head and then her own. No one she knew had hair. Most wore a headscarf to protect themselves from the sun. Banners fluttered above her and peddlers shouted their wares; the sound of haggling and laughter was infectious. Even Tusat skipped along.

Father stopped at a small stand, paying a precious clay coin for a small stick of honey solidified with rice flour. Breaking it in half, he gave the sticky sweet to the girls. For the girls, it was an unheard-of delight. Father had been here many times before and knew exactly where he was going. On the far side of the marketplace was a stone dais covered by an awning of red and white. Corrals filled with people cluttered both sides of the dais. A large open space directly in front was also filled with people. These were mostly men. The affluent and pompous sat in sedan chairs on the shoulders of slaves.

Putting Ankh on the ground, Father stopped to talk to another man. Licking the sticky residue from her fingers, Ankh peered into the corral. Sorrow filled the eyes of many of the children peering back at her. She did not hear the clink of clay coins. Nor did she see Father back silently into the crowd and hurry away, his head bowed in sadness. Tusat also was enthralled by the view before them. The man reached down, slipping a knotted rope over Tusat's wrist. Gripping both girls, he shoved them into the corral.

"Father!" shouted Tusat. Fear spread to the littler girl.

"Your Father is gone," the merchant said with a grin showing blackened stubs of teeth. "He has sold you to me and I will sell you to another."

Tusat opened her mouth. Before she could call out again, the merchant brought the back of his hand hard against her face, knocking her to the ground. The other children pressed back from the two. Ankh did not understand this brutality. Her parents did not strike them. When the merchant moved away, she clung tightly to her sister. Neither girl uttered so much as a whimper; they had learned early in life not to show weakness.

Hours ticked around the sundial before the merchant stood before them again. Pulling Tusat away, he dragged her onto the dais and placed her with four other children of about the same size. At a hand signal from a prospective buyer, the merchant shook Tusat out of her tunic. Heedless of her humiliation, he made her turn around, bend over, and squat. He spoke of her strong limbs and straight back. When he at last had his price, he threw her tunic back to her as a handler led her away. Ankh stood frozen against the rails, watching Tusat move away roped together with other girls. Shock and fear drove all thoughts from Ankh's mind. Tusat allowed the jerking rope to guide her steps.

It was late afternoon, most of the occupants of the corrals were gone. A dozen small children remained. Shading his eyes, the merchant surveyed the crowd. Usually, he sold the small children first. They were a noisy disturbance to his business, but his best customer had not yet arrived. On auction day, the Major Domo from the house of Pharaoh Hokakhty habitually arrived early. Today, the banner announcing his presence was only just wending its way through the crowd. The merchant sighed in relief, signing to his handlers to take a small break.

"So, have you had a profitable day, Ahmed?" The Pharaoh's Domo asked.

Bowing low before his better, the merchant merely shrugged his shoulders. "I knew you would come. I have many children today and saved them for your pleasure."

"I need four, maybe five."

"Four? Only four?" Sniveled the merchant as he opened the gate. "There are many. All strong young bodies aching to serve Pharaoh."

From his sedan atop the sweating Nubian slaves, the Domo waved his lash. Each child stood alone, naked in the open space. The swish of the lash moved from side to side, directing their movements. After the last child had been shown, the Domo indicated which group he would take and the merchant approached him to haggle price. Among those accompanying the Domo was an elderly woman and her assistant. On the days he came to buy children, the Domo used the motherly pair to assist in the calm transport of the youngsters. They, with half dozen guards, would wend their way back through the crowd to the Palace. So Ankh left the marketplace. She had been sold twice that day, once by her father, and this time by the merchant. She walked away, leaving childhood behind.

Why her father had deserted her and where her mother was were the only thoughts tumbling through her mind. She was herded into a small group of children, who huddled together even though they were strangers. Poverty had put them there, fear cemented them together.

CHAPTER 2

It was a long walk to the slave entrance of the Palace. The old woman shepherding the children stopped at a public fountain to allow them to drink. The oldest was perhaps six years of age. All were thin and ragged. She walked among them, encouraging them to keep up while watching for the occasional wayward soul. One of the little ones lagged slightly behind, not because she was weak, but because her head flew from side to side, looking at everything around her.

Once inside the Palace gates, the children faced an open washing area used by all who fell within the lower ranks. They were stripped of their rags, given a bath with a strong smelling, oily soap, and had their heads shaved. After they bathed for the second time, they were given a skirted garment to wear. The day had been long, Ankh was hungry and tired. She longed for her mother's comfort. Although her resistance was growing weaker, she slapped at the hand of a slave who directed the children to a stone bench to wait. This did not go unnoticed by the chaperon.

What is this? The old lady wondered.

Aloud, she asked, "Child, why are you rude? Do you wish to feel the sting of the Major Domo's lash?"

Ankh's face crumbled. "No," she whispered. "I am hungry."

"Well, I have already sent Kia-a, my assistant, for your evening meal. I do not think the Domo will be here tonight, so we will eat and then you can sleep."

The rice gruel arrived. Into each bowl, the woman dropped a slice of fruit. "This is a little treat from Pharaoh to welcome you to his home." She sat next to Ankh, whose curiosity was still at work. "Where were you this morning, girl?"

"Home. Home with my father and mother. I have a new baby brother. My father brought my sister and me to the market, but then he became lost." The threat of tears glistened in the little girl's eyes.

"You are not lost now. This is the Palace of Pharaoh. You will live here within his glory." The woman assured her.

The old woman took the children to an empty dormitory room and hurriedly assigned each a pallet for the night. Beyond wearing, Ankh sank down on the hard pallet. Throughout the night, the old woman woke to check on her charges, lingering longest at Ankh's side.

When morning came, each child received another bowl of rice gruel, but this time, there was no fruit. They washed in the fountain, then sat again on the stone bench waiting for the Domo. Swinging her feet, Ankh, rested and fed, gazed about from the bench.

When the Domo arrived, the old woman fell to the ground before him. The children, including Ankh, immediately followed her lead. The Domo sent the biggest boy to the stables. Another went to the kitchens. "Take these two to the gardeners. Asps have claimed many of late."

"Great Domo," the old woman said, trembling at her boldness, "perhaps you could leave one child here?" His haughty stare burned her. Quickly, she finished her request.

"To be trained as a handler. There is much to do."

"You already have an assistant. You do not need another." He strode away, with his retinue following closely. Kia-a offered to take the children to the gardens, but her offer was turned aside. The old woman took each child by hand and they moved down a stone paved corridor.

CHAPTER 3

Overlooking the gardens were terraces filled with exotic blooms. Beyond the terrace were the harems. Spacious rooms housed the wives and concubines of Pharaoh. They were guarded by eunuchs, waited on by tongueless slaves, and ruled by the First Wife. On this day, a battle raged within the harem confines. Not among the silly girls who played in the fountains, or pouting, dusky beauties who waited a summons to the divan of Pharaoh, but a battle in which the First Wife hoped to win her freedom.

On the outer edge of the harem wing, was a room whose ornate vaulted ceiling was its only decor. Forty paces by forty paces with a polished marble floor. This was the birthing room, the place where the children of Pharaoh took their first breath. Embedded in the walls, several metal rings with silken ropes were available if needed by a woman straining through a birth. In the center of the marble floor stood two poles carved of ivory, each was fashioned with slender finger grips to be a grasping tool for the mother-to-be as she squatted in her labors.

The First Wife of Pharaoh held tight to the poles with white knuckled concentration, mind bent on the mission of delivering a son. Two maid servants knelt on either side, offering their support should she need to lean upon them. Another waited behind to catch the child as it fell among the embroidered pillows. None of the women touched the First Wife; it was not allowed. Only one whose rank equaled or was superior to hers could touch the wife of God-on-Earth. Only Pharaoh, and he would not leave his pleasures for mere child-birthing. Instead, he sent his Priests. They stood against one wall chanting and ringing the little bronze bell that First Wife was learning to hate.

This was not her first child. Since the time that she had stopped being Pharaoh's sister to become the First Wife, she had birthed two other children. Both boys, both deformed monsters. She had destroyed the babes; the Priests had destroyed the servants. No other knew. Even Pharaoh did not know. It was a power Yeach and Gai, the Head Priests, could hold over the First Wife should they need it. The promise to First Wife at the time of her marriage to Pharaoh stated should she bear a healthy son, she could turn aside the attentions of God-On-Earth The rest of her life would be spent here in these rooms and gardens, in peace.

She stood momentarily, then stooped. Her legs were cramped, and she was exhausted. "Ra," she prayed, "Let him come soon. Let me not grab that accursed bell to throw it to the bottom of the well." She took another breath, squatted, and pushed mightily. The women who watched grew fearful. Her face was dark red, and she was sweating profusely. It had been many hours. The sudden feeling of her insides exploding forth caused her to stumble. Only the numb fingers wrapped around the ivory poles kept her from crashing down upon the child.

First Wife pried her eyes open. She glanced over her shoulder, her breath came as hard pants that jarred her body. He lay on the pillow. A perfect baby boy. The woman behind chewed the cord in two; still he did not cry. His mother turned, grasping his arm to lift him. One jarring shake and a shrill cry sounded. She put him down while she finished the birthing. Yeach took the baby away while Gai collected the afterbirth. Lying on the cool floor, her flushed body was comforted by the strength offered by solid stone. Weakly, First Wife reached out to touch the two women who still waited.

"Assist me," she whispered. Then dark comfort came to her. Released to do her bidding, the women worked swiftly. After her body was cleaned, she was moved by litter to her private apartment. The way was cleared of other harem occupants, so none saw her weakness. Left among her pillows with only the old woman who had known her since her own birth, First Wife slept until the coming of her husband.

He did not arrive unannounced but sent his Head-man bearing a gift, a brilliant tiara, to celebrate the birth of his son. When Pharaoh came to First Wife, he did not enter through the private door to her chambers. Instead, he strolled through the harem. Every woman, wife or concubine, knew of his pleasure. Many were envious of the son, Pharaoh would accept some day as Regent, even though other sons had been born previously to him. The shrewd smiled behind their veils. They knew First Wife found the coupling with Pharaoh distasteful. Now was a time to design their place in power.

"Greetings, Wife." Pharaoh smiled broadly. First Wife had been prepared carefully. She reclined on silken pillows as though merely resting. Her ornate wig was flawless and a gossamer gown disguised her still swollen body. Lines of charcoal outlined her dark eyes, even her lips were stained in a tempting manner. Smiling languidly, she inclined her head, pointing to the child sleeping peacefully in his basket. The wet nurse fell face down on the floor.

"Your son, my Pharaoh."

"Ah yes. My son. I have waited a long while." He moved casually to the basket. Everyone waited for him to peek at the boy, perhaps even to smile down upon him. No one expected Pharaoh to scoop the infant up. Walking into the sunlight shining through the sheer curtains, he hesitated a half breath before stepping out into the hard light on the terrace. Everyone except First Wife followed Pharaoh. She lay among the cushions, trembling with fear, fingers pressed against her mouth. Did he know her secret?

Pharaoh stood at the railing. The child whimpered in the scorching sun, which was harsh on his sensitive eyes. With a sudden movement, Pharaoh thrust the child up above his head, then spoke, his voice a strong command.

"Behold my son, Egypt."

Returning to the chambers of First Wife, he allowed the nursemaid to take the crying child. Pharaoh moved to the side of First Wife, tenderly touching her cheek. Never did his smile fade, even when she flinched from the brushing touch of his fingers. Though his heart had softened at the sight of the infant, it hardened again against the mother. Only his eyes changed, becoming blacker, smaller, harder.

"Rest Wife, you will be safe here, but here you will stay," he whispered.

He left through the private entrance into the inner hall. His Priests followed, taking with them the basket and nursemaid. Tears gathered in the eyes of First Wife. Her son was gone; perhaps she would never see him again. This was the price she was willing to pay, so she would no longer have to share her sleeping divan with Pharaoh.

CHAPTER 4

Releasing the child's hand, the old woman walked slowly

away. Ankh barely noticed. She and another child had been

brought to a place where the desert had retreated. Here were

splendors beyond her imagination, exotic plants with flowers

that burst forth from every branch while tall palms swayed

gently. Small birds darted after each other or sat singing while

hidden in the lush greenery. Cleverly constructed pens held

animals she had never seen before. All had been given as a

tribute to Pharaoh; all were displayed for his pleasure. Until

mid-afternoon, the two children wandered the huge enclosure

away from the place they had been told to wait, unnoticed by

most, ignored by the rest.

Pharaoh had summoned the Head Keeper of the

Gardens the day before. There would be a great procession in

celebration for a prince had been born. Those who filled their days caring for the green space and its inhabitants worked feverishly. Many guests would be invited. All must be ready. There was no time for two small, ignorant slaves waiting to be trained. In the heat of the day, Ankh and her comrade, Duth-ta, lay napping on the stone benches. Their wanderings had tired them and they were hungry. So, it was the Head Gardner found them. Always short tempered and now anxious over the demands of Pharaoh, he was not pleased. He shouted for his woman. Her running advance was halted by his staff rapping across her shoulders.

"This waste. Do you see this waste?" His voice rose, becoming shrill. "I have four days to prepare for the guests of Pharaoh and two slaves are sleeping in the sun."

This time, when he swung his staff, the woman leaped out of range. Grabbing the two girls, she shook them mightily, hissing, "Brats. Ignorant children. Who left you here? Why wasn't the Dahaba told that you were here?" She cast a crafty smile as she watched the retreating back of the Head Garner. "Do not worry, husband, I will put them to work," she shouted. To the children, she said, "You want to wander about the gardens? You like the flowers? Then I have just the task for you."

A stable of children too small for the heavy toil was kept to be used as walkers. Throughout the gardens were areas of grass or reeds, places where the residents of the Palace wandered at leisure. There was also a man-made lake with tiny barges afloat. As the day warmed sufficiently to awaken the cold-blooded pests, the walkers were sent out to shuffle through the grass as bait for any poisonous reptile that had obtained entry. A particular problem were the asps. Never large, but always deadly, one bite would cause a fast and painful death. Before the wives, concubines, or children of Pharaoh could step into the lush, exotic retreat, the walkers offered themselves to the dangers.

A child bitten would show the gardeners, who followed where danger lay. In death, they would have served their prince. Sometimes the bodies still convulsed as they, along with the bodies of their slithering murderers, were thrown into the river where crocodiles waited. The crocodiles did not care if they fed on human or snake.

Eidod, wife of the Head Keeper of the Garden, oversaw the children assigned the walker's task. When they were not sweeping the garden, they were assigned to assist those bigger and stronger. Dahaba was a rough taskmaster. Often his staff crossed the back of those who were slow to move. Eidod's back was no exception. Dragging the little girls to a shed, she gave each a roughly woven sack and a snaring stick. The sharp "V" at one end and pointed tip at the other would be their protection.

"I don't like snakes." Ankh stated, fearfully throwing the snaring stick down.

"You would rather the love of Pharaoh be bitten?" asked Eidod silkily.

"I do not care." Crossing her arms across her thin chest, Ankh turned away.

Duth-ta whimpered. The snaring stick cracked down across Ankh's shoulders, sending the child into the dirt. Tears filled her eyes just as the sandals of Eidod appeared. Swallowing the hard lump in her throat, Ankh willed herself not to cry.

"Get up." Taking Ankh's hand, Eidod slapped the stick across her palm. She expected to see tears running down the little girl's face, but only an over-bright stare met the taskmaster's eye. "Now let me show you where you will walk."

The sun was well advanced. During the hottest part of the day, neither the temple occupants nor the vipers were a threat except around the lake, where older boys patrolled as they watched for crocodiles. Eidod spent time showing the girls exactly where to walk and how to use the meager tools at their disposal. If the culprit was not a bird or one of the harmless lizards, they were to catch it and place it in their bag. If they saw a snake before it saw them, they could call a gardener for assistance, never looking away lest the snake disappear.

The task was not difficult. Often, they would catch a rat and throw it in the bag already containing a scorpion or two; small humor for the long days of their lives. Eidod taught them the snake charmer song.

Not everyone was lucky. Only a few days passed before

a child was bitten. Ankh and Duth-ta clung together as they watched another girl-child wither in her final agonies before her body was cast in the waste cart bound for the river.

"I will not be bitten. I will not die like that," whispered Ankh as Duth-ta sobbed. Thereafter, when she walked, she no longer saw the beauty but looked for the death.

On the day of the great celebration, the girls were awakened early, then set to sweeping paths when they were not walking. They did not get to see the procession or the magicians, but at the end of the day, each received a half melon and a large portion of flat bread with their gruel. Another generous gift from Pharaoh.

"Do not eat it all," Duth-ta instructed Ankh. "Hide some for tomorrow."

"I am hungry now."

"And you will be hungry tomorrow."

Ankh knew this to be the truth. With a sigh, she wrapped the bread in a piece of rag to hide under a flat rock hidden beneath her bedding. In this manner, she hoped to keep the rats from eating it before she did.

The seasons of Ra came and went. If a child lived to be six or strong enough for other work, then they no longer walked the garden paths but moved on to more difficult duties. Shortly before Ankh stopped walking, she was in the hidden garden when a woman appeared with a small boy. Stepping back into the fronds of a ground palm, Ankh sought to hide. Unable to leave while the pair moved about in the open, she sat watching.

The nursemaid released the hand of the toddler, coaching him to walk to her as she crawled backwards. He giggled merrily as he clutched at her robe. Later, she removed his short skirt of white linen and allowed him to play in the shallow fish pond. He had one lock of hair that grew from the center of his head, a small braid adorned with glittering baubles. The sudden approach of marching feet caused the nursemaid to start. Grabbing up the baby, she wrapped him in her shawl. Fighting to free himself to continue his play, he yelped in pain as one of the baubles caught in the embroidery of her bodice. Swearing to the gods, his caretaker scooped him up and ran away.

After the marching feet passed, Ankh approached the pool. It had been a long while since she had thought of her brother. How big would he be now? She crouched at the water's edge. And her mother? Did she think of Ankh and wonder where she was? The flicker of shiny scales drew her attention. Several fish bobbed back and forth in front of her, curiosity drawing them to an alien object in the pool. Slowly, Ankh reached into the water, her hand brushing against the nosy carp. In her palm she held a shiny bangle—the head of a ram carved from gold that had once adorned the scalp lock of the Prince of Egypt. The air before her danced with a secret she could not discern. Later, she would find a safe place for her treasure.

CHAPTER 5

Elevated from the position of walkers, Ankh and Duth-ta now
spent their days pulling weeds or cleaning up the trimmings
left behind by those who pruned. It was never ending,
strenuous work.

"Ooh, my back," groaned Ankh. Straightening, she
looked across the garden where Duth-ta worked behind two
gardeners wielding short-handled wooden hoes. A rough shove
sent Ankh back to her labors.

"Don't start moaning now, girl. You are too young to
wince like an old woman." Yesta-ah-dah was a strong worker.
Known for the speed and perfection of his work, it was
whispered among the slaves, he would soon be apprenticed to
Dahaba whose present assistant had been offered a chance to
oversee gardens far on the other side of Pharaoh's Palace.

Dahaba was pleased this young man he had selected had been so honored, but the other man was his son and the thought of separation saddened him. Lesteah strolled past, her hips swinging provocatively. Recently, she had been given the task of running messages for Eidod.

Two days before, Eidod had hurried across the pavilion to rain punishment down on one who had not followed exactly the commands of Dahaba. In her haste, she had darted across the marble staircase recently washed. Her foolishness caused her to slip and fall to the floor, crying out in pain as a bone in her leg snapped. Only her kinship to Dahaba protected her. Until she healed, she would lie on her cot and send Lesteah to do her bidding as her husband instructed. Lesteah arched her eyebrows and swung her hips again.

"What do you do here, Morning Blossom?" laughed Yesta-ah-dah, narrowed eyes watching Lesteah's movements.

"Hmm, I did not notice you to be working here." Lesteah lied. Her full mouth framed small, even teeth, her strongest feature. "But I have water. Would you like some?"

Ankh took advantage of Yesta-ah-dah's preoccupation

with the other girl to rest. This flower bed, which lay beneath the windows of the First Wife, needed constant attention. Many hours were spent plucking unworthy blades from the lawn. Hot sun burned Ankh's skin on. This was the hottest part of the day, and no shade trees grew here. When boredom overtook her thoughts, she returned her attention to the flirtatious pair.

"How do you know this?" Yesta-ah-da queried.

Laughing, Lesteah continued walking through the garden. Her steps were short and periodically she spun in a small, graceful circle that kept her close to where Yesta-ah-da stood.

"I am there, awaiting her every whim. I hear it all." Lesteah sighed in feigned boredom. "Shall I tell you what the old woman said when she was told you would replace her favorite son?"

The quarreling of two women on the terrace above sent the slave girl running while the man and girl bent back to their tasks. Shrewdly, Ankh thought of what she had heard. Lesteah was stupid, a whore who used tricks of gossip to gain the attention of men. Even though her years were few, Ankh knew.

The time she had spent in the slave quarters had not dampened her natural curiosity. She watched everyone and listened too much. Rarely did Ankh bring attention to herself by offering information.

Afternoon moved to evening as, tired and dirty, she made her way to the dormitory. In passing the hovel shared by Dahaba and Eidod, she heard the injured woman call out. "Lesteah, come here. Lesteah."

Looking about, Ankh saw no one. Quickly, she ran to the fountain to rinse the dust of the day from her face and hands. She could do nothing about the dirt-smudged tunic. Bowing respectfully, she entered Eidod's lodging.

"I am sorry, Mistress, to be of bother, but I heard your call and came to see if you needed help." Her demeanor was meek, humble.

"What do you do here?" Eidod was in great pain and her voice reflected all.

"I did not see Lesteah. I thought I could help," the child replied, backing towards the door.

"Yech, she has been gone a long while to fetch food. I am thirsty and the draught left by the accursed physician is out of my reach." Eidod's grumbling traveled between anger and whine.

Ankh rushed across the dirt floor to the rickety wicker table. Grasping a flask of water and the clay vial, she returned to Eidod. After Eidod consumed the contents of the vial, Ankh left her sipping from the flask. When Ankh arrived at the area assigned for the slaves to be fed, she found Lesteah engaged in conversation with another young man. Though it was on the tip of her tongue to mention Eidod's plight, she did not do so.

All were fed from a community pot, though some, like Dahaba, took their meals back to the rooms they occupied. The only difference between overseer and slave here was the amount they were allowed to eat and the special treats the overseer had sometimes garnered from the gardens.

Ankh ate in silence, watching Lesteah while Duth-ta chattered. It was a long while before the older girl left with Eidod and Dahaba's evening meal. Ankh also noted Lesteah did not walk alone into the darkness. Chewing thoughtfully on a last bite of overcooked and rubbery gruel, Ankh considered what she saw.

The next morning, Ankh rose early and scrubbed in the fountain before donning a clean tunic from the pile provided for all. She hurried through the dormitory. She checked quickly to assure Lesteah still slept, then she ran to the gatehouse.

"Good morning, Mistress." Her voice was clear but muted. "I only stopped to see if you were already one with the morning and perhaps needed something for your comfort." In truth, Ankh had paused at the curtained doorway to listen until the harsh grumbling of Eidod was heard.

"Awake! I have been awake for hours." Eidod raised herself on her elbows. "Where is that stupid girl, Lesteah? She is supposed to attend to me. She should have been here long ago."

In an even fainter voice, Ankh replied. "She still lies upon her pallet." Modestly casting her eyes downward, she continued. "It was very late last night when she and…the boy returned." Though the words were simple, the implication was clear.

Eidod's face grew darker. Even as she opened her mouth to spew her anger, Ankh approached her bedside.

"I brought you fresh water. And two pomegranates. I am sorry, Mistress. I took them from the ground because I am too short to reach the branches." She allowed sorrow to darken her eyes for only a moment before she continued. "But I could bring back some breakfast for you. I could even get you bread. Perhaps one stronger than I could carry you out into the sun for a short time." Her eager smile was infectious.

"Yes." sighed the old woman. "Go."

Knowing she would only have a short time, Ankh sped off. Not far from the hut, she met two bigger boys who were already moving towards the elephant garden. After telling them that Eidod wished to be moved outside and that she would tell the Head Gardner of their help, Ankh sent them back the way she had come. At the slave kitchen she approached one cook she knew well and explained she needed food for Eidod, confiding also that, though she had been treated harshly before, perhaps if she did well her lot would improve. The jolly, round eunuch prepared a small basket with fruit and a bowl of gruel that showed bits of gristle floating on top. With a half loaf of unleavened bread balanced on top, Ankh returned.

Eidod had indeed been moved outside. She was pleased at the generous respite spread before her. Bowing away, Ankh returned to the gardens below the harem where she would work that day. There was no time left for her to eat. As she hurried along, Ankh passed Lesteah strolling with her new admirer.

"What do you stare at?" the coarse young woman demanded of Ankh.

Unaware that she had stopped and was watching the pair, Ankh wet her lips nervously. She was about to tread on to dangerous ground. "I, I didn't want to disturb you, but I have seen Eidod this morning."

"What do you talk of? Why would you have seen that old crone?"

"Only in passing." Shrugging her shoulders, Ankh continued with her half-truth. "She is sitting under the great olive tree with her morning meal spread before her."

"How is she outside? Who would have fed her?" Lesteah's eyes widened in fear.

"I am uncertain. I only know I heard her complain of no melon." Ankh took a tentative step on her way while Lesteah chewed on her bottom lip and wrung her hands. The new beau was forgotten.

"She wanted melon? Perhaps if I bring her some, she will not concern herself with my tardiness." Rushing back the way she had come, Lesteah left the others. Watching her go, Ankh knew there was no melon to be had that day in the kitchens. From there, the older girl would have to run to the gardens. She would be very late.

* * *

The evening meal was long past. Freshly scrubbed, Ankh moved along the path towards the hut of Eidod. For two days she had kept away and avoided Lesteah, as well. Tonight, the moon shone full, revealing Lesteah's admirer pacing before the dormitory. Ankh trembled in fear. Carrying a large piece of sweetened bread scavenged from the kitchens, she tiptoed into the gloom.

"Mistress Eidod?" she whispered.

A harsh voice tinged with sleep answered. "Wh

is there? Light the lamp so I can see."

There was a rustling in the straw, assuring Ankh that Eidod still lay on her mat. The smell of incense and urine was heavy in the air. The brightening lamp revealed the old woman lying in the dirty straw and blinking blindly.

"I brought you a sweet. I thought you would still be outside since it is so warm."

"I can't go alone, now can I?"

Placing the treat out of the old woman's reach, the girl moved to the mat. The smell was overpowering. "Your mat needs to be changed. You will need to bathe." With a heavy sigh, Ankh spoke as an adult to a child, "I will help you."

Moving Eidod from the hut to a seat beneath the gently waving palm was no simple task. Ankh was a small girl. Only her stubborn attitude completed their journey. She ran to the fountain across the courtyard and returned with a cracked basin and a jar of clean water. Leaving Eidod to bathe herself, the youngster tugged the soiled mat outside and left it beside the doorway. Hurrying to the dormitory she shared with others of her cast, she looked for anyone she could cajole or bully into helping her. She returned with a clean mat, a tunic large enough to slide over Eidod's frame, and by using future treats to come as a bribe, Duh-ta. With her friend's aide, they moved the moaning woman back into her hut.

"I have had no supper. Where is Lesteah? Why does she not come?"

Fear grew in Ankh's heart. Eidod sounded so weak. Her husband was not here, for Eidod's sharp tongue frequently sent him to the company of another.

"Phew, the smell in here is still bad. Perhaps you should burn incense," suggested Duh-ta before she left. While Eidod devoured the bit of food Ankh had brought, Ankh scoured the hut looking for an incense burner. In a small brass pot, she found a tiny stub. The smell of sandalwood rose in the air. To Ankh's surprise, Eidod slept. The exhausted child returned to her own mat, quickly tumbling into dreamless rest.

* * *

The next morning, Ankh knelt wearily among the hibiscus, plucking weeds and yawning. A commotion on the path halted her small efforts. Dahaba moved along the paving, his staff beating a rapid tattoo. Held by a fierce pinch in the soft under flesh of her arm was Lesteah. Pain contorted her face, ravaging her features. She sobbed, begging him to release her. They slowed but did not stop at the edge of the path.

"You," Dahaba said, his staff pointed in Ankh's direction. "Were you in my hut last eve?" At her frightened nod, he continued. "Then you know the way. Go there and stay until I return." He yanked at his captive as he continued toward the rear of the compound.

"Slimy, filthy brat," screamed Lesteah. "You foul breath of dirt. You did this to me, you liar. OW, ow, please master, you are hurting me, please."

Dahaba's staff cracked across the girl's chest. Lesteah cried out again in pain, then as those kneeling among the greenery watched, the pair disappeared around the next bend, and finally, the rapping of wood on the stone path and the sobbing whine faded.

Dread flowed through Ankh. What had she done?

"Go," whispered her companions. "Go before he returns, and we are all doomed."

Ankh ran through the shimmering heat. Sweat trickled down her back as her fear that she'd be the next to feel the sharp pain of Dahaba's staff grew. In her mad dash for safety, she passed Eidod in the courtyard, sitting once more propped against the olive tree. The old woman explained that, with Lesteah gone, Ankh would now fetch and carry for the gardener's wife.

Ankh quickly learned that any statement preceded by "It is the command of Eidod…" brought instant results. Though her raised status bolstered her confidence, it came with shadows. She feared vengeance from Lesteah or her companions, but she never again saw the other girl and the admirers who had followed the ill-fated woman so closely avoided Ankh.

CHAPTER 6

Ankh's elevated status took her into places she had never been before. She walked in the enclosure filled with the caged wild beasts, which she admired and pitied at the same time. She patted the great stallions of Pharaoh but stayed a respectable distance from the haughty, spitting camels. Every garden was opened to her, every outbuilding, the lake, the barns, the granary, and the kitchens. Doing Eidod's bidding proved to be a simple job. Shrewd sense taught her the wisdom of keeping her eyes open so she could bring information to Eidod before her mistress asked, and then to quickly follow the orders given to her. She also learned the subtle trick of implying that the little treats Eidod preferred would mean less scrutiny. She often brought back a handful of dates or a sticky sesame cake. The elder allowed her time to wander around unfettered since she knew that in doing so, Ankh would gather more gossip.

Early in the day, most went to their duties diligently.
Later, the heat caused some to seek a hidden spot to rest. This
was the time Ankh most often wandered the garden paths.
Although she rarely concerned herself with finding the hiding
places, she noted who she did not see working. One day, her
path brought her to the edge of the stable gate. Two boys who
should have been weeding among the fruit trees were absent,
but the shrill giggling of their voices could be heard among the
leaves in the trees. Finally, one spied Ankh peering up into the
branches. When she did not leave quickly, they became
nervous and dropped to the ground. One grabbed up his basket
and bent back to his task. The other sized the girl up.

"What do you stare at, boy?" Ankh asked, confident the
power of Eidod would protect her.

"I heard you were a bully. But you are merely a small
child." He sneered.

"I am not a bully. I merely do the bidding of my
mistress."

"Eidod is not a mistress. She is a slave."

"Yes," Ankh said with a sly smile. "You are right. She is a slave, but she is different from you and I. She lives well, answering only to one appointed by Pharaoh."

The boy walked slowly around her for a few moments. She wondered if he would attack her. Bodies occasionally were found floating in the man-made lake.

"What if I told you, I know more than Eidod?" he boasted. "That I can read and I have heard that she cannot."

"You can…read?" Ankh asked hesitantly.

"Yes. You know; the glyphs." He waved absently at the stone gate.

Her gazed followed his pointing arm. There the stone walls gaped to allow space for the metal gates, which usually created a solid barrier, were now standing open. Not knowing what the boy meant by glyphs, she continued to stare while she waited for insight.

The boy grew haughty. Walking to the wall, he pointed to a row of pictures sculpted on the wall to the left of the gate.

"Here, little girl. These are glyphs. They tell what you will find within and where you will find it." When Ankh continued to stare stupidly, he moved closer to the wall. "I can read this, can you?"

"No," she admitted. "Tell me what you read."

He studied the wall for a moment, then pointed out one of the symbols.

"This is stables, so I know what is inside the gate. This is horse and this is right, so if I go through the gates, then to the right, I will find the horses. Here is camel, and this is left. The path to the left will take me to the camels. Then wild beasts…," he pointed to another, "…are to the left again."

Having wandered those paths, she knew this was a truth, but was unsure if he was telling her honestly or was merely playing a game.

Leaving her still trying to decipher the glyphs, he laughed at her ignorance and moved back to his work.

Ankh stood in the shade of the fruit trees for a while longer. An old man pulling a cart of straw came through the gate. Stepping up to him, she halted his progress.

"Gentle father," she said, respectfully looking at the ground. "I wish to know what this sign means." She pointed to the glyph the boy had called stable.

"That is the sign for stable," he wheezed. Grateful for a chance to rest, he leaned against his cart. "Why do you ask?"

"Can you read more?" She stared at the row of glyphs.

"No. Well, yes. I know the sign for horse because I work with the horses and so need to find them." Laughing through a mouth vacant of teeth, he added, "But I have been here a long time and could find the horses from anywhere."

Ankh reached up her hand, but the glyphs were far out of her reach.

"Can everyone read them?" she whispered.

"Most cannot." Shrugging, the old man picking up the handles to his cart. "Only if you are shown, I suppose. If you have a need. There are many. Only Pharaoh knows them all."

Long after he was gone, Ankh hurried back to Eidod. She had been gone several hours and the old woman was cranky. Ankh sighed, knowing it was going to take much to appease her. To the surprise of both, the younger son of Eidod and Dahaba came, bringing food and seeking time to visit with his parents, which allowed Ankh to return to the wall.

Smoothing a place in the sand, she copied the glyphs she knew until she was certain they would never leave her mind. Through the next several days, she realized much she had considered decorative carvings were actually glyphs. The few she knew made no sense among the many she saw.

Eidod was in a foul mood. Everything she could reach, she threw. She demanded to be carried outside. Dahaba had long since escaped her wrath, so Ankh brought a strong young man to assist her mistress. Seated beneath the olive tree, the old woman had nothing to throw, so she resorted to screaming at all she could see. Ankh brought a pitcher of water, which Eidod immediately threw to the ground. The young girl's shoulders slumped. There was much to do, and Eidod's anger was of no assistance. A hand touched her shoulder. Ankh turned to find a bent old woman behind her.

"Fetch another pitcher of water, girl," said the crone. "Ah, you poor old woman," she cajoled. "Why do you act like one of the spoiled children from the Palace?"

Eidod looked up in surprise. "Austa! Oh, Austa, they are sending my son away. Already one is gone and now the other goes." Huge tears rolled down Eidod's face.

Ankh ran to fill the pitcher before going to the kitchen area to beg for a treat for her mistress and the woman who had appeared from the air, bringing peace to the gardens.

"Austa. Are you sure she was called Austa?" questioned the friendly cook as he slyly slid a stale crust into her hand.

"Yes, do you know her? I have never seen her before."

"Eidod had a sister. I think her name was Austa. She was taken to work in the Palace. I do not think she has left its walls in twenty years. She would be old now. I don't think she ever had children; only Eidod did."

Taking the crust and the pitcher, Ankh returned to the olive tree. She found Austa comforting her sister. The visit lasted past the noon hour, then the old woman took up her cane and hobbled away. Eidod was quiet for the rest of the day.

Though Ankh was from afar and had no family within the Palace. It was not so for all of those who served Pharaoh. Eidod had been born on the Palace grounds and knew little of the outside world; she had siblings and children who worked and lived among God's chosen. Her favorite, a sister older by one year, Austa, worked as a cloth keeper and seamstress for the women of Pharaoh.

To Ankh's frustration, it was proving difficult to find others who knew the meaning of more of the glyphs. She had asked many, but most knew none. Even Eidod knew only a few. The old woman was wary of why Ankh wanted to know more. "It is not wise to try to know all that Pharaoh knows."

"There are so many. I could never know them all. I only wish to better serve you." Ankh's mind raced as she searched for the words to appease Eidod. "You are so good to me. I want to help, but am afraid." She ended in a small voice.

"Afraid of what?"

"The Palace grounds are so large. What if I get lost? I could never find my way back." Her lie brought laughter.

"Don't worry, you scrawny little thing. If you get lost, you will surely be sent back because you are too weak to keep."

Ankh bit the inside of her lip. It would not do to irritate Eidod now that she was able to hobble around on her own.

Soon Eidod would not need the assistance of another. Today she moved slowly through the fruit trees while Ankh followed, carrying a small basket. When it was half full, Eidod covered the fruit with a ragged cloth.

Eidod would send fruits or vegetables in secret to her sister; in return, Austa would send scraps of cloth. If this contraband was illegal, neither appeared to take notice.

"I want you to take this to Austa," Eidod directed Ankh. "She is in the Queen's Palace. Keep the fruit covered and stay away from any of the Palace occupants. You are merely a garden slave; you have no business in the Palace. It would not go well for you if you became cheeky with one above you."

"I cannot take this to your sister," Ankh replied, panic edging her words. She stared with eyes as big as oranges. "I have never been inside the Palace and would never find her."

Pharaoh's primary residence covered over two hundred acres. Every doorway was guarded. Every one who entered was questioned. The few slaves Ankh had ever seen working in the Palace wore gleaming white garments and looked freshly scrubbed. In her shift of unbleached linen, she would surely stand out.

"Austa works within the harem. The rooms where she works are also the rooms she lives in. On the far side of the gardens is an entrance near to that area. Do not worry. I will give you exact directions. When you approach the guards, tell them I sent you and that you want to go to Austa. Lesteah traveled many times into the Palace for me with no problems. You have taken her place, so now I send you." Eidod drew a map for Ankh in the sand. Though Eidod had seen her sister only a few times over the years, they had always kept in touch through a runner. Eidod's tattoo would not allow her access into the Palace so she sent another.

CHAPTER 7

The Queen's Palace was a free-standing structure of four levels; each level had a high vaulted ceiling and structural specifics for its use. On the outer side it abutted the river, where wide, shallow steps led from the water's edge to the River Terrace. This was the coolest spot in the Palace.

At ground level, it contained potted plants, comfortable seats, and was obtainable only if the Queen's good graces allowed. Open on three sides between thick pillars, shrouded by sheer gauzy draperies that rustled with the barest breeze, it was a place of quiet reflection. The river's edge was shrouded in the same gauze cloud, allowing a woman privacy if she wished to go to the waters. On the outer edge, guards protected those who belonged to Pharaoh. No matter how hot the sun, burly men stood shoulder to shoulder, halting any who would pause. They also effectively kept the harem residents within.

On the courtyard side of this level, was an area designated for kitchens or other areas needed by the armies of slaves. Underground tunnels led from one building to another. An intricate aqueduct system provided and removed the copious amounts of water used in the Palaces.

At the fountain, Ankh scrubbed herself as Eidod had directed. The dust of the garden paths was washed away and with it went the fear Ankh felt upon entering the House of Pharaoh. She crept down the marble corridors, bravery growing, bowing profusely at every encounter. The laughter of other slaves dogged her footsteps. When at last she found Austa, her ability to breathe returned.

"Child!" the crone said with a smile. "It appears you have gained a level in Eidod's eyes." Austa beckoned Ankh into her inner sanctum. Bolts of fabrics, sheer or shiny, every color of the entire world, it seemed, were stacked about. On a dais stood a wooden frame sheathed in a half-completed garment. "What are you called?" The old woman's voice interrupted Ankh's awe.

"Ankh. I have no other name and am of the freemen."

"Hmm. I think when you tell others your name, that is all you should say," cautioned Austa. Merely nodding in agreement, the child reached out a tentative hand to a bolt of peacock blue silk.

"Careful, girl, do not soil that piece. The First Wife has ordered it be kept for her only."

At the end of their brief visit, Austa gave Ankh a tiny bundle of fabric scraps for Eidod, then sent her back to the outside world.

Now the Palace also became a place Ankh traveled. It was enough to enter the shrine to God-On-Earth. Though given an exact route to follow with instructions not to deviate, it was not many trips before she wandered. There were also those she chose to speak with. Her open, smiling face brought friends easily. Life was idyllic for the months that followed, but as in the course of life beyond the palace walls, here too, some things changed.

* * *

Dahaba was old when Ankh first met him. Now he was

older still. His bent body and wizened chest had become hard with a growing cough. As Eidod grew stronger, her husband weakened. In the world of Pharaoh, if a slave lived to be old and useless, he would be sold to a poorer man. There was no ease in old age, only the knowledge that a new master, one who could not afford a younger, stronger worker, would add a heavier burden until the gods called. For Dahaba, that future was not a threat. The seer came, read his stones, and offered a token to Ra and Hades for the crossing of the River Styx on the old man's behalf.

Another gardener was assigned Dahaba's place even as the old man lay on his mat dying. The boy-child of his replacement sat waiting across the courtyard, watching the hut and chewing on a piece of straw. When the dark bird of death landed, the boy would run to his father. Then their family, slaves all, would swoop down to take custody of the hut. Eidod had already collected her few possessions. She would go to live with her son and his family and continue to work there. She was also ready.

Ankh sat in the doorway, watching the boy. She had

listened as the seer worked her charms with Dahaba, telling him his time of rest was near. Standing quietly behind Eidod, Ankh had eavesdropped as her mistress and the gardening son had petitioned for the old woman to join his family when his father had passed into the hands of the gods. Not once a word had been spoken of her future.

The new gardener had a family. He would not need her. Behind where she sat, in the shadows of the hut, Dahaba's rattling breath rose in a fit of hard coughing. Ankh could hear Eidod weep. Fear clutched the girl's belly. Crawling to the old woman's side, she reached out and tugged at the woman's dusty robe.

"Mistress," whispered Ankh, "what of me?"

"Huh? You?" Frowning, Eidod stared at the child blankly. She did not care. Ankh was just another slave, but deep in the back of her mind a small voice reminded her that when Lesteah, who Eidod had loved as a daughter, had deserted her, this child had seen to her comfort. For several minutes, she continued to chew on nearly toothless gums. Exhausted sighs preceded every movement as the old woman took up a small woven bowl into which she placed a few withered pieces of fruit. On a scrap of parchment, she made her mark, handing all to Ankh.

"Take this to my sister. Tell her I have said you served me well. Tell her of my husband. Perhaps she will have a place for you." Kneeling once more beside the dying old man, she added, "if she does not, the Domo will tell you your place."

Ankh hurried from the hut, fearful the angel of death would accidentally suck the breath of her life while claiming Dahaba. She heard the wailing of Eidod as Dahaba breathed his last. At the sound, she ran faster across the courtyard. She did not see the youth stand and run for his father.

CHAPTER 8

The power of Austa was far greater than that of her sister
Eidod. When Ankh presented herself, Austa merely assigned
her work. Ankh never heard the Head Keeper of the Queen's
Fabrics ask permission to keep the youngster or explain a need
to do so. Ankh's relief was great, but though she thought living
within the Palace would be far better than the hot and dusty
gardens, she found working for the seamstress to be more
difficult. The bolts of fabric were heavy, the storage rooms
dusty and hot, with no breeze allowed to enter. She was young
with a strong back. Therefore, the heavy work found its way to
her. No longer did she freely mix with other slaves or freeman.
Those who worked for Austa slept where they worked, with
merely a single blanket to soften the marble floors. An ancient
woman who did the fine stitching the Queen demanded cooked

their single meal on a brazier set out on the small balcony.

"I should have taken my chances with the new gardener." Ankh softly complained to herself.

Her skin was gritty and sweat ran burning into her eyes. In the two years she had been there, she had worked from before light until long after the six other women had gone to their nightly rest. Austa was a stitcher of renowned abilities. She had served the wife of Pharaoh when the Queen had been still a maiden and been promoted to the Keeper of the Queen's Fabrics shortly after the Queen had been married. Austa ruled the enormous vault of fabrics, most of which were gifts from foreign places. Within her rule, where six other stitchers. Each chosen because of their speed and the delicate work they could produce. These women applied bone needle and thread from dawn to dusk, then sat against the balcony wall, eating their gruel while the darkness thickened around them. Ankh, on the other hand, spent her time fetching and carrying. Because none of the six could read, each memorized the name and distinction of each new fabric, they expected Ankh to learn this as well.

In addition to all else she did, Ankh fetched water,

emptied cess-pots, and moved mountains of material. Austa would not let outside slaves invade her private world. So Ankh filled every spare moment, sweeping up the desert sand that filtered or shaking more sand out of the fabrics. Though she did not yet visit the rooms of the harem or wield a needle, the young girl listened avidly to the gossip that swirled continually around her and learned of the women they served. Who was who, which ones received special treats from the Pharaoh or more often from the First Wife. She also learned how Austa plied her wits into the will of others.

During the hottest part of the year, the household of Pharaoh moved to the River Palace. The distance was perhaps only ten miles outside the edges of the, but the site was secluded in a narrow valley that encircled the river. The tall sand cliffs offered respite from the hot, still air. Wives and concubines traveled with Pharaoh, but except for a favored few, the children were left behind. The River Palace had its own staff of slaves. Only those specifically selected by their lord or mistresses were carried away in the ox drawn wooden carts that followed the ornate sedan chairs. The Queen did not take her seamstress, but the request to attend her could be expected at any time.

During one of Austa's trips to the summer residence, Ankh leaned against a relatively cool stone balustrade, wiping the sweat from her face.

"Huh. Are you tired of fetching swatches and threads?" One crone smacked her lips together in laughter.

"I am blessed to live in the house of Pharaoh," replied Ankh. She had learned the importance of watching her words. Caning was the preferred method of treating insolence. Many times, Ankh had felt the long rod fall against her back. Her left eyebrow was split by a diagonal scar brought on by the heat and Austa's temper. Ankh had selected an inopportune time to answer carelessly. Even as the fresh response to her mistress's order slipped through her lips, the ever-present cane crashed against her face.

"Huh," said Yalinew, who was Austa's lieutenant, and the stitcher assigned to fancy embroidery work. "You think you are blessed? Before we did as you do, every one of us. Before long, the old Tuyat will go to Ra. Who will take her place?" The old woman's sly words caught the girl's attention. Yalinew was given to providing information cryptically. "We will each grow with her death. But we will need another to help with the sewing. Will it be you? Do you stitch? Or will you continue as you do now while another comes to take up the duties left without hands?"

"I do not stitch." Ankh crept closer to the crone. "But I could learn. I am not a mindless fool." Tentatively, she reached out, touching the other woman's tunic. "You could teach me, Yalinew. I have heard it said your work is fine and well respected."

"Why would I teach you? It would be easier to find one who already knows." Yalinew rubbed her gums with a crooked finger.

"Perhaps there is something I could offer you, a trade." smiled Ankh. Her smile evaporated as quickly as a drop of water was sucked in by the desert sand. She had nothing to offer. The old woman knew it.

"What will you give to me? Your ragged blanket?" Yalinew gazed up into the evening sky. The smile that played on her lips drew Ankh closer. On this side of the Palace the balconies overhung the holding pens of exotic animals which, each in their own turn, were allowed to cavort in the enclosure below the harem. Here they were kept shaded. Only the odor of feces and old straw spoke of their proximity. Wrinkling her nose against the rising stench, Yalinew reached out to shove Ankh away. "Do not look so forlorn, small one. It will be your turn to learn soon. I have heard Austa speak of it. If you are wise, remember to work hard. All will be well. But if you tell her I spoke of this before her, I will fill your blanket with fleas and biting flies."

Again, the old woman's lips came together in mirth. This time, Ankh laughed with her as they sat together and waited for a night breeze.

Indeed, true to what Yalinew had said, Austa raised Ankh to the level of apprentice. Another scrawny girl came to take Ankh's place, though Ankh still found herself fetching when the old ones were too busy to work with her. Austa was fanatical about to not wasting the beautiful cloth. Daily, she instructed Ankh on sharpening her bone needles, the use of the cutting tools, and always the measuring string; a braided section of threads whose equally spaced knots were used to mark the fabric accurately before the garments were cut.

"I see you have no new bruises so you must be listening better when Austa instructs you," said Yalinew, who was rarely out of humor.

Ankh enjoyed the time she spent learning from the elder woman. "It does no good to be too eager. I make mistakes and she watches me like a hawk." Peering at a sample Yalinew had given her to copy, Ankh paused. "I did not know if I really wanted to sit sewing all day, but I like this best." From Yalinew, she'd learned to embroider clever designs which would garnish garments. It had been a pleasant surprise to Ankh, as well as a great wonder to everyone else, that she did so well in this particular area. "I would do this all the time; I do not care to learn to measure and cut. Nor do I care to hem, hem, hem."

"Huh, you need to know it all to be good. Even I do things I do not care about. It makes better that which I love." Looking over her shoulder, she whispered. "You have done better than was thought. Tomorrow Austa will go to the market. The cloth traders will be there. I go, Chinata goes. I hear you may go as well."

Ankh dropped her work in surprise and stared at Yalinew.

"Shh, quiet. I tell you only because it gives me pleasure to take the wind from Austa's bellow. Be quiet!"

Austa and Yalinew shared a common heritage and with it came a language none of the other women spoke. Often, they talked together to the exclusion of everyone else. When Ankh followed Austa up one level into the harem loaded with garments to be tried or fabrics to be selected, she heard many strange tongues. Austa seemed to understand them all.

Perhaps, Ankh thought, *I should learn also.* But the trick of languages escaped her. Only when the women looked upon her, tall, erect, blooming into womanhood, did she know what they spoke of, though she did not know what they said.

Yalinew's voice cut into Ankh's thoughts. "Tomorrow, you will have to be veiled to go outside the Palace walls. You will speak to no one. You will remember your place, for we will travel as part of the Major Domo's entourage. If you displease him, he will take it out on Austa. Then none of us will be able to save you from her wrath."

Ankh cowered slightly inside even as excitement burned brighter. She had not been out of the Palace since first she had walked through the gates.

CHAPTER 9

Ankh had entered a new phase of life within the Palace.
Perhaps because she was young where the others were old,
perhaps because she was eager to learn, unafraid of the
unknown, or perhaps merely because she grew to be a beautiful
young woman with a generous and friendly spirit. Soon she
accompanied Austa to the marketplace regularly. Old Yalinew
gladly stayed behind. When the harem was in residence, she
often went- up the smooth marble steps, today with the
measuring string, tomorrow swirling about while draped in a
new shimmering, iridescent fabric for the women to admire
and vie for. It was not until the next hot season that she
traveled to the summer palace.

The Queen's summons had come in the late afternoon.
Austa's women worked late into the night gathering all that

would be needed to satisfy the Royal temper through the days Austa would be in attendance.

"We will have to be ready to leave by first light," grunted Austa, obviously tired. Circles of sweat under her arms and breast showed her exertions. Yalinew shook with exhaustion. Austa's shrewd eyes watched the old woman's tottering steps. "I think you will accompany me, Ankh. Yalinew has much work to finish here."

"With you? I will go with you?" Ankh's voice rose in excitement. Yalinew sighed in gratitude.

Secretly pleased at the girl's response, Austa chided her none the less. "Shh, do not shout. Remember, we are going to a place of rest and meditation. Now go, wash, bundle what you will need. We leave early."

They rode in a covered ox-cart. Ankh moved constantly from one side to the other, interested in everything they passed. When they left the city behind, Austa ordered Ankh to sit still. The day was already hot and Austa was tired. The brief night had left the older woman nauseous and with a sour temper. Behind them, another cart followed with their stores, all surrounded by the Pharaoh's guards. All knew these women were from the Pharaoh's household. Some stared, others dropped their heads in respect, while Ankh spun from one exciting scene to another. Though the distance was not far it, would take several hours for the plodding oxen to arrive. Austa napped but Ankh struck up a whispered conversation with the elderly guard who walked beside the cart. He saw her as an amusing child. The morning sped past. Her giggling stories would be a treat he would remember for his old woman when next he saw her.

The summer palace differed greatly from where they had come. It seemed to be built right into the high cliffs. Merely two levels, it covered a vast area. The banking was narrow, so though beautiful potted plants and trees were set about, the gardens were lacking in the wide straight paths found at the winter palace. Here, walkers moved around botanical displays often out of sight from where they had been seconds before. Wide marble or mosaic steps led down to the water's edge where the river Nile, wide and shallow here, drifted lazily past. Large, ornate barges humbled small reed boats that dotted the river. Ankh panted with excitement, amusing even the dour Austa.

While Austa went to the Queen, Ankh supervised the unloading of the goods. Their assigned area was small. Ankh knew she would love it. A small noise caused her to turn from a basket of jumbled threads. A boy of perhaps sixteen stood behind her. Dressed in a short white tunic, he was fair of face with skin the color of thick honey, muscular but not tall. From the top of his shaved head, one long strand of hair hung down across his shoulder. A ribbon of gold entwined throughout.

"Hello," Ankh said with a smile.

The boy paused, then spoke with just the edge of disdain. "I have not seen you here before."

"No, we just arrived. The Queen summoned us. What a beautiful place. The journey was wonderful." Giddy with her own pleasure, Ankh did not see the boy's watchful eyes scrutinize her. A smile appeared on his face.

"The Queen? Well, we will surely see you about."

With that, the boy left, and Ankh forgot him as she moved to the windows overlooking the river.

Three days passed before she saw him again. She had gone ahead of Austa with her arms full of swatches for the Queen to assign for the various other wives' garments. The boy was in the hall and she smiled as she passed.

"Are you still so excited to be here?" he asked

"Yes, I love it all." Her joy was short-lived as Austa rushed up behind her, grabbing the back of Ankh's gown and forcing her to her knees.

"Bow," she hissed. "Bow before the son of Pharaoh, He who one day will rule."

The Prince, this was the Prince! Neferet's only child. Ra would surely strike her down. Ankh crumbled to the floor, crushing the cloth beneath her, trembling in fear. The boy laughed lightly as he walked away.

"I did not know," Ankh wept to Austa as she gathered up the swatches.

The old woman angrily yanked them away from her. "Go wash your face. You must learn to be more careful or your life will be very short."

Ankh ran back to the haven, closing the door and

leaning against it as her trembling knees gave out. How could she not have known? She had seen him before when he was a toddler, though for the last few years he had studied with the Priests in the Temple of Ra. For Ankh, the rest of their visit was on pins and needles, concerned she may have blundered and might never return.

On their return to the capitol, the seamstresses worked until late in the night, finishing the garments ordered by the Queen. Day after day, they stitched until their fingers bled. The time had come to return to the summer palace. This time, four women went. The excitement in the harem as they unpacked their goods was tremendous. Reclining on her divan, the Queen would survey each garment, touching the fabric, stroking it almost lovingly, then calling for two or three women and finally passing it to a new owner.

"Huh, like she did not know who would receive that vest before she had it made." Huffed Yalinew.

"Maybe she did not. Maybe it is just a gift." Ankh beamed, as did the recipients of the Queen's blessing. Her face was flushed, eyes sparkling merrily.

"Do not be stupid. She knew. It is her game." Grunting, Yalinew pulled another pair of sheer trousers from a basket.

Over her bent back, Ankh saw the Prince enter the room. In this place where men were not allowed, he came and went freely. After drifting through the group of women as he accepted their greetings, he perched on a cushion where his mother could lovingly touch his shoulder. Only then did his gaze rest upon Ankh. She blushed to be caught staring, looking away as he smiled in her direction.

The days after the gift giving were busy. Adjustments were made to garments, a tuck here, and a seam re-stitched there. Wives who had received the gift of a length of fabric vied to have their new garments made first. Ankh seemed to be forever trotting along the corridor, the cool marble smooth beneath her feet. Several times she had seen the Prince but, on this day, he seemed to be lingering as he perched on the balustrade with only his ever-present companion for company. The son of his father and one of his lesser wives, Sibes, patiently followed everywhere Prince Kaakhsi went.

"Hello. Yes, I am talking to you." Strong white teeth

flashed. Moving smoothly, Kaakhsi stepped in Ankh's path. She immediately dropped to her knees, but not before she noticed his grace and pretty looks. "No, no. Stand. Walk with me."

Sibes reached for her basket, moving back to the stone railing. Kaakhsi led the way down into the potted garden. Among the columns, a bench had been placed, so those seated would be shaded from the glaring sun or the eyes of others. Here they sat for an hour while Kaakhsi convinced Ankh to talk to him, regaling her with tales of his own.

They met there twice more before the seamstresses left. Quietly Ankh sat in the cart remembering his voice, how he had known she would be sensitive and earnest, telling her that his life was pointless, boring because there was no one he could talk to. Kaakhsi had cautioned her about speaking of their meetings to others whose jealousy would destroy their friendship. Their friendship! He had selected her to be his friend. She was filled with pride at the thought, and blushed at the memory of his warm fingers resting on her arm. Her heart was bursting with the want to share their friendship with someone, perhaps Yalinew, but Kaakhsi had made her vow to stay silent.

Only Sibes knew. Ankh frowned. She neither liked nor trusted the Prince's half-brother. When Kaakhsi was earnest in finding a place, they would be safe from the eyes of any who might destroy their friendship. Sibes stood behind his Prince. The halfling watched with cold, laughing eyes brimming with cruelty and hinting of a dark secret, Ankh believed to be his own. Sibes was the asp hiding among the flowers. Even when Kaakhsi sent him away, he did not go far. When their short time was through, Sibes rushed Kaakhsi away, his laughter carrying back to Ankh tainting the edge of her glow.

CHAPTER 10

The ensuing months flew past. The family of Pharaoh returned.
Kaakhsi was again in the temple, receiving the training his
father had ordered. Then, without warning, Sibes approached
Ankh as she traveled from the kitchens. He had a message
from the Prince. This palace was much busier than the summer
palace, but there was a place where they could meet that others
would not find them. Near the audience chamber, there were
several small rooms for private meetings. When dusk had
fallen, Sibes would meet her in the corridor of fountains. Then
he would take her to a meeting with Kaakhsi. She was ecstatic.
Over the following weeks, she met him there several times.

Ankh no longer needed Sibes to show her the way.
Silently, she let herself into the antechamber. Normally, many
lanterns glowed, but tonight there were none. "Kaakhsi?"

Across the room, a woven rack of gold held six candles, the only light. Behind the rack, gossamer curtains waved in the faint breeze, fluttering the candles.

"Here, beloved, I am here."

Ankh's heart fluttered as the candles had. She was stunned. He had called her beloved. What did he mean? She moved slowly toward his voice. A low divan had been placed in the arch leading onto the balcony where the cool evening breeze would wash over it. There Kaakhsi reclined casually. Gracefully, he rose, extending his hand for hers, drawing the suddenly shy girl to the arch. Far above the balcony rail, the moon, large and full, shone down upon them.

"Do you see the face of the moon? It smiles upon us, knowing it is the time for love to be declared," he whispered. "For me to tell you how you stir my heart and for me to hear that you also feel the strength of love."

Kaakhsi's arms encircled Ankh, and she leaned against his naked chest, feeling the warmth of his skin and the beating of his heart. Before this moment, she had known nothing of love, but now, she knew everything.

"How can you love me?" she whispered. "You are a prince. I am…a slave."

"My heart does not care that you are a slave; it does not care that I am a prince. It knows only that I hunger for you when you are elsewhere. Have you not noticed I search you out?" He smiled into her eyes.

She had noticed but thought it a game and was now ashamed. Lowering her gaze, she pushed gently away from him. He allowed her to wander, stopping her before she stepped out onto the balcony.

Holding both her hands with one of his, Kaakhsi poured wine from a small carafe into two jeweled goblets. Only when he was through did he release her. "This, my Perfect Lily, will seal our devotion to each other. Our promise of the night and the days to follow."

Ankh gazed up into his eyes. Her look searching, even as her heart beat wildly in her chest. A tiny voice said no, but there was a screaming in her ears saying yes, yes, and again, yes. Ankh sipped from the goblet but a tart bite remained on her tongue. She turned her head aside.

"No, you cannot avoid my offering, beloved." Kaakhsi laughed, moving closer, and she felt the heat.

Again, Ankh's heart bounded. She allowed him to tip the goblet up, taking the remaining wine in one long sip.

Turning from her, he placed both goblets, one untouched, back on to the table. As she stood as still as a statue of pure alabaster, he moved around her, rubbing her arms, the back of her neck. His kisses, light and airy, fell at random, growing more urgent.

Shuddering with the intensity of the feelings that seemed to grow from low in her stomach, a small groan escaped Ankh's lips. Was that her? Had she made that animal sound? She felt confused and reached out, looking for the solidarity of Kaakhsi's body. Her fingers found only emptiness, but she was not concerned. Warmth spread through her, contentment, peace, and then, a new feeling, a longing grew. As if with a mind of their own, her suddenly wet palms ghosted across her breasts, down her stomach, ending at her thighs. Her gown was gone, but the thought barely penetrated her mind. Her hands moved without her will, moving slowly towards the meeting place of her thighs. She stood alone, swaying as the palms did in the evening breeze.

Kaakhsi stood back, watching her movements. He, too, was naked. Now his smile was not kind or loving. Ankh would have seen power had she but opened her eyes. Before the girl, drugged and unknowing, moved to pleasure herself, he took her hands and pulled her back to the low divan. She lay before him, writhing, arching, fighting for the release of her hands. When he released her, rolling her onto her stomach, it was only to pull her hips up and against him. Powerfully, he entered her. Senseless, she did not even scream. Sated, he left her lying unconscious when he was done.

Hidden in the shadows while he waited for his Prince, Sibes bore silent witness to Kaakhsi's brutality. With the use of his thumb and the first two fingers of his right hand, Sibes strove to release his own desire, casually at first, then with heightened need. During all, he also watched the corridor door. Sibes knew Kaakhsi had been ordered by his father to partake only of the seasoned women who would teach him the subtle arts of love. Pharaoh did not want his son to spawn bastards throughout the city, weakening their regal line. The son, however, was not interested in women who did not offer conquest. At last Kaakhsi's desire wore thin and, finally sated, he left Ankh and slid unconscious to the floor.

Sibes wrapped a cloak about Kaakhsi's naked body, then removed him through a hidden door. The pathway to Kaakhsi's rooms was long, only the late hour kept their journey secret. Even in those places where they moved in public corridors, they passed no one. Kaakhsi would have gladly lain on the floor and succumbed to sleep, but his comrade dragged him onward.

The hard morning sun burned her eyes, waking Ankh. There was a metallic taste in her mouth. Her head ached behind belief. She cast her eyes about. *Where am I?* she wondered. *How did I come here?* Then she remembered Kaakhsi and his declaration of devotion.

Pulling herself up quickly proved to be an error. The lights in her head burst into new a flame as vomit rose in her throat. Standing on shaky legs, Ankh knew she had to get back to the stitching room. She would be hard pressed to explain why she was on the balcony, and Austa would be angry. Only when she retrieved her tunic did Ankh become aware of the bruises and bite marks on her body, the dried blood between her thighs. She was not sure what had happened the night before, but she knew it was evil. But the Prince of Ra could do no evil, therefore she alone was guilty of something she could not even remember.

Creeping back to her pallet, she moaned to Yalinew that she was ill. Austa had gone to meet with the cloth merchants and Yalinew took pity on the despair in Ankh's voice and left the girl alone. When all were busy elsewhere, Ankh rose, scrubbing the filth from her body, weeping in shame.

When next Sibes appeared with a summons for Ankh, she went hesitantly.

"Why," she asked Kaakhsi, "did I feel as though my body was not my own? How is it I remembered nothing and found myself where I should not have been?"

Listening to her story, Kaakhsi's arms encircled her. He held her tightly.

"Poor Lily," he murmured. "Do you not remember me telling you of my love? Or how you responded with yours, offering your body in tribute? My Beloved." She remembered Kaakhsi calling her beloved. She remembered there were lilies. Or were there?

"I was ill throughout the day," she whispered. "It was not in a way I had ever been before."

"Poor Lily," Kaakhsi crooned. "I will have my own tasters alerted. You may have consumed something unfit. I don't know. Had I been aware, I would have rushed to your side with my own personal physician." He smoothed her hair. "My poor, most precious girl."

Kaakhsi offered a jeweled goblet. There was an odor, a taste on her tongue, that made her hesitate.

Perhaps this is where the illness came from, she thought.

With a smile he put the goblet to his mouth and made as to drink. A small rivulet of wine dribbled onto his chin. Laughing, he wiped it away with the back of his hand. "Will you not share what I have to offer, Beloved? The bread that I eat, the wine that I drink, I would share with you." He wiped his hand across his chin. She took the goblet and looked into the wine, never noticing he had not swallowed. Then Ankh smiled up at him and accepted his offering.

Twice more she succumbed to his trickery until finally, using Kaakhsi's own trickery against him. She held the wine in her mouth and spat it behind the divan when his attention was drawn to her naked body. It was a sly trick, but unaccustomed to the use of drugs, Ankh did not realize that merely by holding the liquid within her mouth for a few minutes, she would consume enough to render her defenses useless. Even as her body betrayed her, her mind saw a frightening truth. She had always survived by the use of her own wits. Now she knew she had been blinded by the promise of that which she had always coveted—love. No longer would she drink or eat what he offered.

"No, my heart's desire. I do not need the wine. I wish only the taste of your lips. The warmth of your body, the beating of your heart." Laying her head against his chest, she did not see the frown furrow his brow. "You have spoken of the days before us, and I go willingly."

Kaakhsi stayed with her for only a short while that night. She was not the wanton woman he desired, but a clinging cat who had merely stumbled through the motions.

As Kaakhsi strode angrily along the corridor, Sibes asked, "So, are we done with her?" He received only a curt nod in response.

CHAPTER 11

As the days passed, the strange sickness Ankh had experienced since her last night with Kaakhsi increased. She went to the garden seeking the physician, an aged woman who had the knowledge of cures and worked there among the slaves. Walking up behind her, the old woman grasped the girl's breast, making her cry out in pain. Running arthritic hands over ribs to the flat pallet of stomach only to dig deep into the soft flesh, she caused still more pain.

"Ha," cackled the hag, emptying Ankh's offering into her pocket, "there is nothing wrong with you. You are young, there will be no problem. Your man will be well pleased." When Ankh did not respond, the woman added, "You are with child, probably a son."

Bowed in despair, Ankh walked away. Her mouth was

dry. A child! Even slaves had pride. How would she explain bearing a child when she had not been assigned to a man, when she did not have a husband or an earnest lover? Only Kaakhsi. What would he say when she told him she had allowed this to happen? He was the Crown Prince of Egypt. Yet he loved her; he had told her this. It had been many days since last she had seen him, days he had undoubtedly spent at the Temple in the company of priests and scholars.

"Huh, the Queen is bewitched by her son. He comes and goes. She does not know he wanders among his father's women so casually." Austa returned from the harem jingling the coins the Queen had tossed her for a particularly fine piece of work. Yalinew deftly caught the one tossed to her. Later, she would hide her treasure. It took much to remain calm as Ankh turned to the triumphant Austa.

"The Prince is back?" Ankh asked, swallowing the rising lump of hysteria."He is done with his learning?" Though she tried to sound merely curious, her knees were shaking. She slid to the floor, burying her hands in a stack of fabric.

"No, he is just here for the Harvest Moon festivities; he

studies still. But he must learn the Pharaoh's place too." Austa was not interested in the son of Neferet, only in the bolts of cloth that were in her realm.

Ankh prowled the open windows. Any errand that would take her from the rooms of fabric and stitching to a place where she might see Kaakhsi was welcomed. Her wanderings brought her to the Hall of Fountains in Pharaoh's Palace. Throughout the length of the open-air corridor, one fountain followed another. Black marble to green onyx, from simple form to extravagant carvings. Each a gift to Pharaoh. Many had clever innovations in their making. In an alcove near the far end was a small, plain sandstone fountain. It was called Fountain of Tears, due mostly to the tear-shaped basin created for bathing. The design was also often called a Maiden's Pool.

Kneeling hidden behind the stone carving, Ankh wiggled her fingers in the water, stroking its smooth surface. In an area so calm and quiet, she was hoping the swirl and gurgle of water music would soothe her worries. Suddenly, the quiet was disturbed by the sound of running feet. She turned and stepped from her shadowed alcove just as Sibes pounded into view.

"Kaakhsi! Ho, Kaakhsi!" Sibes' voice echoed through the hall.

Sibes called out again as he closed on the Prince who had just cornered a young girl. With a snarl, the Prince turned to look back at him, which allowed the girl to dart from her corner. She dodged around the Prince and scurried past Sibes, a terrified look on her face as she passed him.

"Kaakhsi!" Ankh called out in surprise. Moving into the center of the hallway, she almost collided with Sibes. The Prince's servant grabbed her arm and steadied her. When she regained her balance and looked again at Kaakhsi, he was glaring down the long corridor the girl had disappeared into, a look of outrage on his face.

Thank the gods, I have finally found him, Ankh thought as she moved toward him.

From past experience, Sibes could see the storm rising. Cutting between the Prince and Ankh, he tried to head off what was about to happen.

"Master, I have searched for you every day," Ankh told

the Prince, the look on her face hopeful and happy. "I've had thoughts you might be sick, or—."

"Why?" Kaakhsi's bitter tone shocked Ankh into silence.

"Why?" she finally managed to say, the word heavy with confusion.

"Why would you search for me?"

The harsh tone of his voice set Ankh atremble. "You have not sought me out. I-I have a need to speak to you."

Sibes paced nervously mere feet away.

"And why would I, the Prince of Egypt, seek out a slave wench?"

Kaakhsi's caustic words stunned Ankh. Tears began to gather in her eyes. "But you love me. You told me you love me." Her voice failed as his stony stare grew colder. Slowly, she began to realize the situation she was in. The possibility that he had lied. The gut-wrenching thought that he'd only used those loving words as a foil grew in her mind. Past the painful swelling of her heart rising into her throat, she forced the tears down and her back straight. She had always been taller than he, now she tilted her head down towards him. For this moment, she would speak what was in her mind, in her heart, even if it cost her life.

"Prince Kaakhsi, I sought your presence that I might tell you ..." Pausing to wet her lips, she continued, her voice cold as the night wind. "... that you have sired a child. And that child grows within me."

Kaakhsi froze in mid-step. The soft murmur of nearby voices warned of others approaching. Grabbing Ankh roughly, his fingers pinched the soft flesh of her upper arm as he dragged her down the side staircase, forcing her deep into the rows of columns.

"You dare accuse me when any man you have lain with could carry the guilt of your bastard." He hissed.

"I have lain with no other," she whispered. Twisting away, she wanted to hide before her tears fell.

Ignoring Ankh's distress, Kaakhsi held her fast, his mind filled with desperate thoughts. He knew his father would be furious and that the Priests would make good their threat for an immediate marriage. There had to be a solution. There had to be! It was not uncommon for slaves to carry the brats of their masters, but Pharaoh had been explicit in his demand that Kaakhsi was to lay only with those presented by the Priests.

Exhaling through his teeth, his lips pulled back in a smile bordering on grimace. His tight grip on Ankh relaxed to a caress that still did not release her. "My pretty lily, you have caught me unaware." Though his lips smiled, his eyes did not.

Shuddering with fear at the look of naked hate in his eyes, Ankh collapsed onto a nearby stone bench. Would he kill her? Was it within his powers to drag her, with the help of Sibes, into the desert, leaving her body deserted on the sand? Or would he just leave her lying here? She could not know Kaakhsi lacked imagination; his only thought was the anger of his father. "Does anyone else know of this secret you share with me?" His words meant to provide himself with time to think.

"Only the physician." Immediately, Ankh knew these words were a mistake.

Though Kaakhsi appeared not to hear her last words, Sibes, who lay cowering against a pillar, obviously did. "M-mmaster!" Sibes he stuttered, springing upright.

Ankh turned, eyes dark with fear towards him.

"Master, there is a way," Sibes offered.

Still wrapped in a desperate mental search for an excuse his father would accept, Kaakhsi did not hear Sibes' words. His grip on Ankh loosened as he considered one foolish excuse after another, only to conclude even Great Ra could not protect him from his father's wrath.

Ankh began to inch away from the pacing Prince, but Sibes blocked her escape. "Which physician?" He demanded.

"One in the garden. I do not know which one or her name. I was sick and went for a potion to heal me. I did not know." Ankh felt herself babbling. Swallowing hard, she fought to regain control of her emotions. There would be no saving herself if she did not.

She knew Sibes was wise in the ways of the common people. He would know there were ways to rid oneself of an inopportune brat. He'd also know that one slave was much like another and rarely were their deaths noticed. But before he could offer his knowledge to Kaakhsi, the Prince spun around.

"Go." He ordered, his voice shaking as his body trembled with the inner terror he was feeling. "Go back to your place. I will come soon. I need to approach Pharaoh carefully for him to accept you."

Ankh and Sibes stared with open mouths. The Prince would tell Pharaoh? Unbelievable.

"Kaakhsi. Listen to me …" Sibes implored, hurrying after the Prince.

But Kaakhsi ignored him, turning to hurry across the corridor and through an open entry to an outside garden. Ankh rose from the bench and quickly scurried away in search of Austa and relative safety.

At the edge of the pavilion, Sibes turned back, his intent to order Ankh to remain until they returned, but she was gone. Frowning, he squinted against the harsh light. When he at last discerned that she had run away, he went back to Kaakhsi, but the other boy was gone. Sibes collapsed on the steps. He knew death hovered soon in his future.

Mindlessly, Kaakhsi moved along the path. His arrival at the stables was not intended, but it did not surprise him. Yes, here was an answer. He would ride long and hard. His anger would boil away. Riding always relaxed him. It would offer a chance for him think without the cursed babbling of others.

In short order, his favorite horse was made ready for him. It was a young stallion of Arabian descent, whose spirit and power were said to match that of any other in all of Egypt. Pounding along the pathways without heed of others, Kaakhsi burst through the enormous wooden gates and out into the desert beyond. That the prince rode away alone was noted by only a few, then forgotten as they returned to the work that always waited.

Riding hard, Kaakhsi bore his heels into the horse's flanks. The short whip he carried flashed again and again. Deeper into the searing heat, he rode. Eventually, foam flecked the animal's muzzle and Kaakhsi realized the stallion was thirsty and growing tired.

The steed crested a dune to find the opposite side had fallen away. The animal reared, trying to rid itself of the lash. Kaakhsi caught at the horse's mane, losing his seat as the dune caved again. Both horse and rider rolled down the mountain of sand, crashing to the bottom. Whinnying in pain, the stallion stumbled to his feet and limped a short distance away, dragging his rider, dead and tangled in the reins.

It was dusk the next day before they were found. The Prince's body was born back to the Palace, the dead horse left on the desert floor.

That evening, Ankh stayed hidden in a secluded corner of Austa's room. Her thoughts in turmoil, she held back the cries of anguish that longed to escape from her throat as she struggled with the shocking news that had swept the Palace.

Kaakhsi could not be dead. He was young and destined to be Pharaoh one day. He was the one she loved.

An extensive search had commenced when a stable master had reported the young Prince had not returned by darkness. Ankh had been sure he merely hid himself away while his anger boiled. The whole city had looked for their Prince.

When the faithful bore their tragic burden back to the Palace, Kaakhsi's body was taken to the temple where only Pharaoh would see. It was so badly damaged it would drive the

Queen to madness to view him. Ash-covered mourners walked the corridors, wailing and spreading incense.

Ankh stayed hidden among the fabrics. Unable to think or plan, she was not missed by any other.

CHAPTER 12

Sibes huddled in his mother's embrace, weeping against her breast. He was going to die; his name was on the list of those who would be sent with the Prince to Ra. A temple was being prepared even as the embalmers worked. Treasure would be collected so that everything Kaakhsi would need in the next world would be buried with him. There, just as here, his half-brother Sibes would attend him.

"Please, Mother," he sobbed, "please, I do not want to die."

She rocked him silently, her own tears falling on to his dark head. No one came near her. She was a woman of violent temper and this was her son, born before the Prince but never possessing his father's heart.

"It's not my fault," Sibes cried out.

Adion shushed him. They both knew it was only the

fault of the headstrong Prince that he was dead.

"It was the girl," Sibes continued. "The Priest told him to stay away, but he thought he knew so much. When she told him she would birth his child, he became so angry."

Startled, his mother pulled him up to her eye level. "What girl? What child?"

Fear kept Sibes silent.

Adion's face was a dark, ugly shade of red. Words hissed from between her teeth. "Answer me. If you want me to save your life, then tell me everything you know."

The desperation and anger in his mother's voice broke Sibes' silence and his words tumbled out. He spoke of the Prince's dalliance with the slave girls forbidden to him. After, he listed everyone he could remember, but he spoke most of Ankh, of the drugs used to keep her and the others pliant. He spoke of the last time he had seen Kaakhsi, of what Ankh had said before the Prince ran off.

Stone-faced, his mother listened. When Sibes was through, she rose and carefully washed her face and repaired her charcoal eyeliner. Finally dressed in her most modest attire, she left her son huddled on the floor with fear in his eyes, and she left their home.

Adion had been Pharaoh's favorite until Neferet caught his eye, and then his heart. Younger by several years and more learned, Neferet had become Queen and Adion's place in the Palace had diminished. Wives and concubines that Adion had hitherto snubbed laughed in her face. So, it was that in the years that followed Adion, had worked just beneath the surface to discredit the Queen. But the more generous and popular Neferet had gone on. Her son moved ahead of all others, while Sibes had been regulated to the errand boy for the Prince.

At the door to the Queen's private chambers, Adion was stopped by the elderly servant who guarded Neferet's rooms and told she must first send a message. Knowing she could trust no one, Adion refused. Pushing the old woman aside, Adion hurried forward, dropping to the floor several paces away from where the grieving Queen lay. Slowly Adion crawled forward, the bejeweled bodice of her robe scratching against the marble floor. Each sob from the Queen caused Adion to cringe. But she knew what must be done if her own child was to live.

The old nursemaid left the door to stand protectively by her Queen as the mother of Sibes crept closer. Neither the look of alarm on the old woman's face nor the agitated flutter of her withered hands halted Adion's quest. As she inched forward, Adion repeated the names assigned to the Queen over and over, titles that for many years she had refused to utter.

Deep in despair, the heartbroken mother of the fallen Prince did not notice Adion's arrival until her groping hands tugged urgently on the rough weave of the Queen's mourning clothing. "Go away." Neferet pleaded, her voice rough from hours of wailing.

"I cannot go away. I must speak and try to save my son," Adion replied.

"Save your son? Why should your son be saved while mine is dead? Was not your son supposed to attend to mine? To stay with him and rid him of any demons that would cause him to lose his life?" Anger rolled through the Queen, a blaze that consumed and was welcomed. Rising to sit above Adion, the Queen unknowingly placed herself in easier reach.

Adion did not hesitate. Pushing aside the old woman who'd scurried closer to protect her Queen, Adion lay her head in the Royal's lap, ignoring the ashes littered on the Queen's robe and fighting stubbornly to keep her place as Neferet tried to push her aside.

"I know you are heartbroken," Adion said, her pleading eyes locking with the Queen's. "We are both mothers. We both love our sons. Great Ra has ordained that your son be buried as a Prince should be, that many slaves and freeman accompany him on his journey. But I am begging you. Do not take my son. Only you can stop Pharaoh from taking him."

The Queen's laugh was harsh, her words tainted with hysteria. "Why should you be left with a son? All these years you have sneered at mine, whittled at my power with your jealous little tricks. Oh yes, I know who you are, what you've done. Do you doubt I would see through you now?"

Again, the Queen tried to shove Adion away, but Sides mother buried her hands in the Queen's robes and hung on. Neferet pulled the wig from Adion's head, then scratched her face. Adion held her place until exhaustion slowed the Queen's fury.

"Your every accusation is right," Adion declared. "I am jealous of who you have become. I was here first, but you became more. Over time, I said things, did things to discredit you, to make others look down upon you. My son was the elder, but never good enough. I do not deny any of these things." She raised her face to the Queen who stared back, shocked but perplexed by the tirade. "You have lost your son. Please do not let the sun set on my life as well. If I can help you, will you make Pharaoh pass Sibes by when the final death toll peals? Please, please, I beg of you."

Beset by the worst fear of her life, her face dark with pain, Adion desperately clutched the Queen's robes as she stared imploringly into the dark eyes of her mistress. The charcoal that had rimmed her eyes ran down across her cheeks.

Long moments passed before the Queen sighed heavily and rose to her feet. Still on her knees, Adion did not release her grip. Tears running down her cheeks, she gazed up at the Queen and the words that were the only chance she might have to gain Neferet's help tumbled out. "I know that when you lose a child, you have lost all the child - unless your son has a son."

"What is this riddle you talk of? Are you mad? I will have you flayed until you are naught but a bloody corpse. Get away from me. Leave me alone," Neferet gave her robe a hard yank, causing Adion to tumble to the floor.

Knowing this might be her last chance, Adion cast all caution to the winds. "I do not speak in riddles. Kaakhsi defied his father and cast his lot. He has a child."

Neferet began shaking. Before Adion could reach up to her or the serving woman could grasp her, the Queen fell to the floor, violent tremors running through her body.

"Bring wine," Adion ordered, wrapping her arms around the Queen. God help her if the Queen died. Whispering urgently, she told the Chief Wife of Pharaoh everything she knew, everything but the girl's name.

Long hours of the day passed while Neferet bombarded Adion with a multitude of questions trying to understand. At last, in an effort to confirm her revelation, Adion sent for Sibes.

Sibes cowered before the Queen, answering each

question with a rush of words. Doubting but hopeful, the Queen eventually sent the old woman to summon her physician, a man she knew she could trust without fear. Sibes was sent to fetch the girls he'd spoken of.

As they arrived, the girls were shown into a small side chamber then brought forward to be examined by the Queen's physician. Neferet's hopes died as her anger rose when, one by one, he declared that none were with child.

"You have tricked me. You have made me a fool," Neferet hissed. "I will have him killed while you watch. There will be no mercy, only agony."

Sibes gasped in fear. His gaze locked on his mother.

Adion lifted her head and delivered the final disclosure of her plan. "There is another girl."

"What? Is this another trick?"

"No, another girl," Adion declared. Her eyes locked with the Queen's for a long time, then she turned her head and gazed through the fading light across the balcony to the oncoming night. There was nothing left to say. Her ploy would work or her son would die.

Neferet's gaze shifted to the pallid boy groveling at her feet. He was not beautiful as her son had been. His skin was blotchy and pock-marked. His shoulders were rounded. He smelled of sweat and fear.

As the Queen's gaze ran over him, he nodded slightly and whispered, "My mother speaks the truth." Then he hung his head and crept nearer to his mother.

A kaleidoscope of emotions crossed the Queen's face. Anger, doubt, hope. And finally she spoke. "Bring her to me."

Ready to obey any command from a Royal, Sibes began to turn. Adion's swift grasp of his arm stopped him in his tracks.

Adion's gaze turned back to the Queen. Her head lifted. "I have been honest with you to prove this is real. Now the game changes. You wish for the last girl and the gift she carries within her body. I wish for my son to live." Adion stood firm, unmovable, while the silence grew.

"Bring her to me," the Queen finally said. "If it is as you say, you may send your son from here. By my direction, he can be sent to the Priest. They can protect him from the wishes of Pharaoh. Sibes will not be with you, but he will live."

Adion released her hold on Sibes. She gave her son a slight nod, and he bolted from the Queen's chamber.

* * *

Full of fear, Ankh knelt humbly before Kaakhsi's mother, the Queen, the chosen woman of Pharaoh. Ankh knew she had committed a terrible sin for which her life could be default. Her mind was a jumble of confusion and her fears grew with each new thought that whirled through her mind. There had to be a single reason she should live; but she could not find it.

The old servant woman stood silently behind Ankh while Neferet's personal physician lingered just beyond the light of the flickering lamps and Sibes and his mother stood silently in another shadowed corner.

Ankh's eyes were focused on the Queen's feet, but when the rustle of her gown indicated she had turned, the girl raised her eyes. She saw the worried old woman attending the Queen, and the frown when she was caught looking. There was a distinguished man on the other side of the Queen. His robes and the acrid incense he carried identified him as a medicine man or a physician. From further behind where she knelt, Ankh heard the shuffle of feet. A quick peek revealed two others standing in the shadows.

A woman, she thought, *and a boy? No, a skinny man.* Her attention was drawn back to the Queen.

Finally, a silent motion from Neferet summoned the physician. He hurried forward to do his Queen's bidding, handing off to the old woman the dangling incense burner he'd been holding. He examined Ankh minutely for a long time, taking her behind a screen and having her disrobe. Then reclaimed the incense burner and walked three times around the girl, enveloping her with pungent smoke, believed to wash away any lies she might carry. Ankh sneezed as the smoke invaded her nostrils. The Queen and the old woman held silk scarves over their mouths and noses. Every time Ankh sneezed, the physician paused, waving the incense burner until her eyes watered.

Neferet watched the girl standing silently. The Queen

was wise to the ways of intrigue and wondered if this was a plot to save Sibes. "Has another from the Palace devised this ruse drawing in you, an innocent, to protect him? Were you offered freedom, riches to perpetrate this lie?" Neferet leaned towards Ankh, her manner threatening.

Pride bubbled up in Ankh's throat. Though exhausted, she stiffened her spine and lifted her chin. "This is no trick. I am not a slave; I was born a freeman. Even if I had been offered riches, I would not play to your emotions, your love of your son and your hope you had not lost him entirely. If you forced me to leave here, no one will know the secret of where this child came. I ask nothing of you, Great Lady. I did not come to you. I was brought by one who has always worked his nasty greed within these walls." Intent on the eyes of Neferet, Ankh did not notice the sudden movement of the woman in the shadows. "Sibes followed the Prince, living on the dregs of the Prince's life, that which was left after the Precious One had passed," Ankh continued. "Sibes is evil in a way I do not understand. A coward without the ability for an original thought."

Sibes' mother shook with rage, and Neferet hid her smile behind a silken scarf she rubbed on her cheeks, her son's scarf, his scent, her memory.

Standing, the Queen descended to where Ankh stood. At the Queen's approach, Ankh dropped to her knees, waiting while the Queen circled her. Dismissing the physician, Neferet spoke for the first time to the woman seated in the shadows. "Go. Our deal is sealed."

Ankh's darting eyes picked out the movement of the veiled woman hidden in the shadows. As Sibes raced from the room, she realized who he was and released a hissing breath.

Sibes was unaware and uncaring of Ankh's response to the revelation of his identity. He had one thought to live. Racing from the room, he ran until he was standing before the temple priests. Dropping to the ground, he babbled, drooling and weeping as he did so, and also offering the tribute his mother had provided. Sibes would stay and the priests would keep her jewels.

In the Queen's chamber, they waited in silence until Adion was gone. The elderly slave standing behind the Queen was her head woman, even in old age a tall, strong-looking Nubian. Orders were given in a tongue Ankh did not understand. The slave stepped outside the lattice door where curtains of silk hung for privacy. Because the room was long and narrow, Ankh could only hear the murmur of voices but was unable to decipher what was said. The old slave returned and stood silently, waiting. Once again, Queen Neferet returned to Ankh.

"You will remain here for the rest of the night. This is Panhsjet. She will stay with you. There will be others. You will be bathed, fed, dressed. They can understand you, but most have had their tongues cut out so they will not answer. I will return for you and my son's child." Briefly, her fingers touched the top of Ankh's head. Then the Queen added, "Know this, however, I have allowed you to speak freely this time because it amused me and... offended one who is not close to me. I will not allow it again." With that, the Queen swept from the room.

It was not until she was told it was time to enter the bath that Ankh stood. She uttered not a word as she followed Panhsjet's directions. She had been saddened and in despair when she entered the Queen's chamber, now she was terrified.

CHAPTER 13

Dawn crested twice while Ankh remained closeted in the Queen's private apartments. Neferet was well known for her sulking moods. No one questioned the barred door. Sharing the head woman's room, which also housed the Queen's special artifacts, Ankh spent her time alone, awaiting the return of the Queen.

Seated just within the bellowing draperies, Ankh watched the sun as it set on her left. She was not allowed onto the balcony even though the harem area was below them on the third level and all the balconies were on the western side. Behind her, a soft cough drew her attention. Panhsjet stood watching.

"Queen Neferet summons," the Nubian said with no preamble.

Reclining on a divan of precious teak padded with

many silken pillows, the Queen looked out over the same courtyard Ankh had been contemplating. This, the fourth level, was occupied fully by the Queen's apartment with its private baths. Usually, a few favorite wives were invited to attend her. Those so selected would stay as residents until they were sent back to the harem.

Though several servants hovered, none had approached her. Ankh was positive Panhsjet made sure of that. The arched windows provided the Queen with visual command over the city, and the river, as well as the Palace courtyards, and a small corner of the Pharaoh's balcony on the opposite building. Tents of brilliant silks shadowed benches set out on the balcony, allowing the Queen to sit in comfort should she wish to watch the wild animals cavorting in their enclosure or the enclosed gardens open to the harem.

"Tell me your story again," demanded Neferet.

Kneeling on the cool stone with downcast eyes, Ankh repeated the now oft-told tale of her rendezvous with Kaakhsi. When it was done, they sat in silence. With a deep, heartfelt sigh, the woman who controlled the apprentice seamstress spoke.

"Pharaoh has many guests. Often Kings and Princes,
come from far lands." Turning her almond-shaped eyes to
Ankh, she said without smiling. "The distance is often long, so
they will stay for many weeks. So, it is now. A Prince from
Niger has come. Like many others, he has brought his family,
his women. Though a few will stay in the guest harem near
him, most will stay here.

"When they enter tomorrow morning, you will enter
with them. It will not matter that they will not know you. What
will matter is that one of the women here may recognize you. I
have given this much thought. You will need to stay veiled, at
least for a while. Remain aloof.

"They will leave in three months' time. When he does,
you will merely remain behind. It is not uncommon for a
woman to be given as a gift. That is how most come here. Your
child will be accepted as just another Royal brat. This will
provide time for me to think, to decide what to do about the
child."

Ankh tilted her head, secretly studying Neferet. Though

her speech was clear, the Queen had an unfocused look. Ankh was sure she could have sat back and made eye contact with no acknowledgment. People spoke of Neferet's ageless beauty, but in the space of days, the Queen seemed to have progressed to a withered, colorless old woman.

Mourning would last for a full year. Garbed in a shapeless tunic of rough weave, covered in ashes, Prince Kaakhsi's mother would grieve the rest of her life.

"Mistress." Ankh spoke in a low tone. "what about Austa?"

"Austa?" Neferet blinked. "She has been told you were sent elsewhere. She and her women will be your greatest threat. Stay far away. I grieve at the thought of sending her away, but for now, I want you where I can watch over and protect you."

Later, when Neferet was at her meditation, Ankh approached Panhsjet. She told Panhsjet of the tiny hidden bag of trinkets that were her life. With only a single glance, the head woman silenced Ankh. But in the morning the silken bag Ankh had fashioned from salvaged scraps appeared among her things.

Via the slaves' corridor behind the baths, Ankh joined the long line of wives and retainers entering the harem. Deftly pushed in their midst, she humbled herself before the Queen then found an alabaster divan in a far corner to stake out for her own. It was near the edge of a window where the hot afternoon sun made itself known. No one had claimed this spot.

Neferet welcomed Pharaoh's guests, speaking briefly of her son, ignoring Ankh. Nearby, Adion stood silently, artfully ignoring Ankh while supporting her Queen. It was a new role for Adion, but a part she played well.

The few articles of clothing the Queen had given Ankh were placed in a chest, one of many that lined the walls of the box room. A shining metal plate attached to the cover announced the owner as Anippe, the name she would be known by from that day forth.

CHAPTER 14

Always a busy place, the harem found itself in chaos. Several groups of diplomats' wives now called it home. People flocked to the city by the thousands for the funeral of Pharaoh's son. The Nigerian Prince had moved his group to a residence he had purchased in the city. Anippe stayed behind, unnoticed.

Spending long periods of time in her rooms, Queen Neferet clung to her mourning attire. Anippe also wanted to respect Kaakhsi by mourning. When she arrived in a group collected by Panhsjet, she spoke haltingly of her desire with Neferet.

"No," Neferet answered. "Others believe you are from away. Why would you give up your life to dress in rags when you have an opportunity to enjoy the same benefits as the wives of Pharaoh? The foreign women will not mourn, even wives of Pharaoh will not last an entire year."

This was a hard truth. Locked away where others could not see them and barraged by the wives of Pharaoh's guests; women who flaunted their best, the wives and concubines of Pharaoh, left behind their rough weave and ashes in a short time.

Only Adion made a halfhearted attempt to console Neferet, perhaps to assuage her own guilt. Anippe watched from afar, and like Neferet, was not convinced of Adion's devotion.

"Why do you sit here so far from the feasting?" asked one concubine, a dark girl, short with a flat nose and tight whorls of hair, as she approached Anippe in a friendly manner.

"I am not hungry." Anippe smiled in reply. An early lesson learned was that a caustic attitude brought more attention. Her time spent in the harem had not passed happily.

"Ha. Women with child are always hungry." A wide grin showed the woman's small, white teeth. "I know. I have two children."

"Two?" Anippe looked at the child-woman in disbelief.

Gazing at the gaggle of children brought from the nursery building across the courtyard, she did not see two who could belong to this girl. The other women had found their own, spending this brief time comparing whose offspring had the most to offer and placing wagers on which would receive notice by Pharaoh.

The dark-skinned beauty giggled anew. "Are you looking for my little fruits?" Merry eyes assessed Anippe. In their dark recesses, a wise fire glowed. "They are not here, my son and daughter. My old master kept them. One to raise to fight, the other to use as a barter." Pridefully, she continued. "I am but fifteen summers. I will have more children."

Taking Anippe's hand, she drew her along. The girl was Marlota, a concubine given from a poorer nation. She had not brought slaves of her own and depended upon those provided in the Palace of Pharaoh to handle the general duties. She had grown capable of caring for herself. Everything she needed was provided by the house of Pharaoh. Ultimately, like everyone else who lived there, she was dependent upon him.

"Are you sad?" Anippe asked, thinking of children left

behind.

"No. My country is poor, but we are proud. I was selected with great honor to come to Pharaoh. Through me, we will have sons that link us. Perhaps one day he will even take me to wife!"

The harem cloister was deep and wide. Archways linked the rooms together, though the only balcony was along the west wall. On the eastern wall were the extensive baths and the case room, as well as the gateway to the Pharaoh's Queen.

Centered in the lattice wall was a double door, the only entrance other than the slave gate. Both were guarded inside and out by six eunuchs.

Anippe and Marlota strolled around the exterior of the rooms. Built to hold three hundred wives and concubines in one communal area, it was molded to create space for individuals to be alone if they so wished. However, even in this open environment, cliques developed amid the fountains, dicing tables, and permanent buffets. Often, groups would form allegiances, staking out an area of their own, dissolving and regrouping anew. The continually changing villages of women shifted among the alabaster lounging divans used for both reposing and sleep.

Vicious fights were the norm, usually settled by Neferet, who now did not care. She had withdrawn. It did not matter that Pharaoh was angry when tales of female battles found a path to his ears. Neferet would not force his wives to mourn, and she could not be consoled. Even the secret knowledge of Anippe's child roused her for only short periods. The Queen could not claim this child outright. Nor after refusing Pharaoh access to her divan for years, could she think of a way to present the coming babe to Pharaoh as her own.

Halting beyond the archway to the baths, the two women peered through the heavy lattice carvings. Across the span of the ten-foot corridor, they could see the colonnades containing rich engravings of Egypt's past. Also visible were the shadowy outlines of ever vigilant guards. Anippe shivered.

"Are you frightened?" Marlota wrapped her slender arm around the growing girth of Anippe's frame.

"Not so frightened as unsure. I miss the freedom I had before I came here."

"Freedom? To move about as you wished?" asked Marlota.

At Anippe's nod, her tiny friend grew owl-eyed.

"I have never before had the freedom I have here," said Marlota, opening her arms to the splendor behind them. "Such an enormous Palace, so much food, the beautiful gardens." When Anippe remained silent, Marlota continued, "There is the river terrace we can explore, or on the roof I hear there are tents and entertainment in the hours before dusk."

"On the roof?" asked Anippe.

"Yes, but all depends on Queen Neferet. Perhaps soon she will return to us. But only if she deems us worthy may we ascend those steps."

CHAPTER 15

Marlota's vivacious demeanor made Anippe laugh. As their

days together grew, a bright glow once again permeated her

skin, replacing the dusty shade of sorrow, her worry creases

began to fade.

Flushed with pleasure at being a knowledgeable guide,

the younger girl wandered the opulent rooms, drawing Anippe

along by the hand. Between the bouts of Marlota's ribald

comments aimed at other residents, they sated hunger with

delectable tidbits from the numerous offerings throughout the

room or surrounded themselves with exotic scented incenses.

As always, at mid-day the children dutifully followed

their nursemaids away, leaving mothers napping on the

damask-carpeted reclining divans. Anippe and Marlota bathed,

then dozed lightly as slaves rubbed perfumed oils onto their young bodies. Eventually, Anippe allowed herself to relax and accept such pampering gratefully.

One late evening brought an unexpected treat—a special warm honeyed wine. Slaves moved from woman to woman, filling jeweled goblets. Even the slaves were being given small wooden cups. The sweet cinnamon odor invited immediate consumption. As the first sip covered her tongue, Anippe's stomach rolled. She had been plagued since conception with a finicky appetite. She put the cup aside.

Sitting upright among the cushions, Anippe yearned for a cooling breeze. Her gaze swept idly over the room. It seemed tonight everyone was settling down quickly, an unusual turn of events. Then there was a sudden whoosh as a sandal flew past her shoulder, causing her to jump. The flying footwear was followed by coarse laughter. One of the women whose divan was near to hers laughed as Anippe turned, surprise evident. This concubine had noted Queen Neferet's generosity to one newly arrived, and proven to be an antagonist. Many times, she verbally baited Anippe. At times, resorted to pinching or sly slaps. When it had become apparent Anippe would not defend herself, the harassment had grown.

In self-defense, Anippe looked for a way to protect herself. While hiding from thrown fruit one day, she crouched behind her divan and unexpectedly noted an opening on the backside which provided a small space masked by draped fabric. It became her secret place. The means of escaping the taunting of other women. Standing, Anippe moved out onto the terrace, drunken laughter following her. When the women's attention was diverted, she crept back into her hiding spot, now comfortably lined with pillows. Though not large, the space was adequate for her needs.

Hours later, Anippe was awakened by the sound of marching feet. When the noise stopped, she listened carefully. Only the unladylike snores of women drugged by the evening's wine offering came to her ears. Masculine laughter seemed to burst from many throats. She gasped, covering her mouth with both hands. Running footsteps rushed closer. There were a few scrabbled screams, and the sound of battle where none should be fought. Something terrible was happening.

There was a solid thump on the floor near where Ankh

lay. An object rolled until it came to rest against the drapery, hiding her. Lifting the covering slightly, Anippe gasped. It was the head of her worst antagonist. Gingerly, she put her foot against the gruesome article, pushing it away.

Silence followed the swift, merciless slaughter of the harem. She could hear those responsible for the mayhem moving about the rooms. Pushing herself further under the bench, Anippe willed her heart not to pound and her lungs not to pant. Before, she had casually hidden from the others. Now she could only hope the huge rooms would not be searched too closely and her hiding place would not be discovered.

Suddenly, the swish of a sword through air and the *thunk* of metal striking bone was followed by a dull thud that Anippe assumed to be a body hitting the floor. Each whispered command made her flinch. Though she tried to force her teeth apart, her aching muscles would not respond. Only when the baby reacted violently to her cramped position did she realize she was alternating between panting and holding her breath.

What is happening? Oh, Isis, she prayed, *do not kill me today*.

Then came the sound of several pairs of shuffling feet crossing the terrace. Forcing her eyes open, Anippe waited fearfully for one who might discover her, fearful thoughts skittering through her mind.

Where are the guards? The eunuchs? Where is Pharaoh?

The footsteps and whispering voices had been silent for a long while. Tremors shaking her body, she dared a peek around the sheltering curtain. The polished floor reflected only faint light. Either the oil lanterns had burned out or been snuffed.

Creeping on hands and knees around the alabaster bench, she lifted her wet palm and found it stained and dripping. Her other hand encountered tangled strands of hair. Scrambling backwards to the wall, she swallowed repeatedly to prevent vomit rising. Smooth silk brushed against her. Stirred by the desert wind, the embroidered draperies enveloped her. Hidden in the fluttering folds and crouched against the stone column, she felt the ghost of something raveling on the wind. The air, once lightly aromatic with cinnamon, clove, and saffron, was dense from the multitude of blood puddles congealed in the heat. The odor, thick and cloying, reminded her of the butchering area she had traveled to for Eidod. It settled in her throat. There was no escaping it. Brief glimpses as gaps in the curtains fluttering in the desert breeze created kaleidoscope pictures.

Lit by a few remaining lanterns, the carnage took on the illusion of a vaguely remembered nightmare. Hopeful that the intruders no longer roamed the harem, Anippe moved slowly into the open. Her first steps were halted as she encountered the eyes of the dead. Averting her gaze, she moved on, hopeful for other survivors. The rancid smells continued to swirl around her, but her will was strong. Pressing her tongue hard against the roof of her mouth, she suppressed the urge to vomit as she crept onward.

Near the base of the staircase leading to the upper chambers, Anippe stared into the surprised face of the First Wife. Another head without a body. No soul shone back through her eyes. Further on, locking the doorway to the apartment First Wife had called home, was her body. Unable to step over it, Anippe moved along the wall in the direction of the main corridor.

I must leave here. Her thoughts flew around within her brain like moths caught in a lantern. She took a few more steps and came to the double doors that marked the entrance. *What if they come back? What if they find me here?* Her tortured mind demanded.

Her small steps towards freedom halted; her legs trembled, and she thought she would fall. If she stepped into the open area of the corridor, there would be no place for her to hide. Better she travel through the small slave corridor.

Bright light still shone through the archway to the baths. The horror of the main rooms was reenacted here, but only a few of the bodies were of the Royal family. Slaves and eunuchs, who had been busy cleaning in preparation for the following morn, lay submerged in pools stained crimson with their blood. Darting across the room to the doors that would offer escape into the smaller side corridor, Anippe gingerly took hold of the brass ring that would pull the portal open. Nothing. She tugged harder, tears welling in her eyes. A thousand times she had seen this same door swing silently inward, allowing a parade of servants in or even harem residents out. It had never failed before. Peering through the carved design, she could see a cross bar, which locked the door on the far side. She could not escape.

Anippe's stumbling feet took her through a different archway into the chest room. Here no bodies lay before her, only the great sandalwood chests that held the possessions of the women of Pharaoh and the tall mirrors of beaten copper that they had pranced before.

In the flickering light, she saw herself, bewildered and afraid. Her sleeping gown was white as the hot center of the mid-day sun, while across her swollen stomach a swath of red marked the nest of her child. When she unconsciously rubbed her abdomen to soothe the babe, she had left behind the traces of blood collected while touching the dead. Her gorge rose and resolve hardened.

Ripping off the gown, she stopped only long enough to wash the last remnants of death from her fingers in a large copper basin before running to the chest with her name on it.

Throwing open the lid, she cast the contents on the floor until, at the bottom; she found the short tunic that had been her slave garb. She yanked the tunic over her head.

The only thing still in the chest was a small fabric packet containing the gold charm she had found in the koi pool years before, and the tiny bits the queen had gifted her. With a thin cotton belt, she strapped the packet on the inside of her upper thigh, never questioning the urge to hide the small square. She had no idea who the intruders were, or how they had entered without someone giving the alarm. But she knew the evil swirling like mist through the lofty rooms would not willingly let her pass.

She re-entered the central room of the harem, where now only the moon lit the interior. Anippe crossed to the terrace and crept along the outer edge, staying below the chest-high railing while she searched for a place she might be able to climb or jump down.

Returning to the chest room where the eyes of the dead did not follow her, she huddled in a corner far from the mirror wall and waited.

The whoosh of an opening door brought her back from a light doze. Peering past the edge of a large chest, Anippe watched as guards ushered slaves into the rooms. Each wore a cloth covering nose and mouth to prevent the spirits of those who had suffered a violent death from gaining entry to another soul. Men ripped down the draperies, rolling bodies into the sheets of cloth after the women had stripped all the valuables from the corpses. A eunuch, taller and blacker than Anippe had ever seen before, moved through the room. The identity of each body he encountered was added to the list the accompanying scribe carried. Drawing closer to the doorway, they paused over another body, trying to decide who the woman could be.

Anippe panted. Did they know she existed? Were they searching for her? Escape seemed impossible. Then she remembered the masked slaves. Nearby was the chest with the name of a minor wife etched on the brass plate. Anippe eased the top open. Among the items was a plain cotton shawl. Ripping a section from the edge, she tied the rag over her face.

There were a few trinkets under the shawl and he scooped them up. Dumping fruit from a woven basket, she threw the trinkets in. Struggling against her own fear, the young woman got to her feet.

"You there, stop!" The man's voice boomed across the room, deep and graveled.

Anippe bowed her head. Sweat ran down her back while shaking fingers gripped the basket in front of her trying to disguise the bulge of her child. The tall eunuch approached her, stopping close enough so she could smell the herbal mix of his bathing salts.

"The cases will be taken just as they are." He looked into her basket. "Take that with you and get back to the others."

Like a beetle in sudden light, Anippe ducked her head and scuttled around him towards the archway. All the while, she kept the basket tight against her stomach.

"Seal this room. Assign a guard," ordered the eunuch.

Anippe's head pulled down into her shoulders as his deep voice boomed behind her. She chanced a quick look and saw the scribe bowing to the ground.

"Yes, Loust," said the scribe.

"Is that all? Have we accounted for everyone?" Loust, obviously a Domo of merit, halted the scribes escape.

The shaking man squinted at his list. "Yes, Loust."

Loust merely grunted as he surveyed the work going on around him. Once again, he stopped the scribe.

"Take them all. Do not bother to separate the slave from the free; they will burn on a common pyre." Finally, Loust moved away. His steps took him to the main entrance where the line of slaves Anippe hid within were ordered aside to allow him passage.

The tension fell from the scribe's shoulders as he followed his master. Anippe burrowed deeper into the line of slaves, their arms filled with goods that had been so highly prized by others only hours earlier. As the slaves hurried to follow the scribe from the room, Loust stopped outside the archway, speaking to a nearby man. His words made her blood run cold and bile rise again in her throat.

"We go now to Pharaoh Brother and tell him the

abomination has been scourged," the Domo boasted. "The Pretender and his accursed whores and bastards are all dead!"

As the group neared a wide staircase at the end of corridor, Anippe slowed her steps and let the Domo and his followers move past her. Leading the way, the Domo and his scribes began to descend the stairs. Bearing the dead and the baskets of goods coldly plucked from previous owners, the parade of slaves clattered after them.

Anippe's hurried backward glance revealed guards had been left stationed at the harem entrance. The belted cords they wore, their badges of allegiance, were not gold on white but black on gold.

Who are they? What is the name of their master? Who is Pharaoh now? She questioned as fear loomed stronger.

"What am I to do? Where will we be safe?" she whispered to the child she carried. "Our world has changed forever."

Frissons of fear were racing through her. Ahead of her there was a loud cry as the line halted amid great amount of confusion as slaves rushed forward. One of those bearing the wood and fabric stretchers stacked high with bodies had slipped on the staircase. Not only had the man tumbled into those below him, but so had the desecrated remains. Men and women both were screaming in the melee. Across the wide corridor was the much small hall that led to the Austa's private world. Ankh looked about. All around her people were crowding closer to the top of the stairs, their horror-filled eyes focused on the scene below.

Slipping between them, she crept across the wider corridor and then raced down the small hall that led to the fabrics vault, praying it might provide her a new place to hide while she tried to think of a plan to save herself.

* * *

The doorway into the stacks of silks and cottons stood ajar. Entering, she slid out of view. No voices came to her; she felt safer already. Moving to the back of the room, she searched for Austa.

In the alcove where the elder had lived, Anippe found only confusion. Cushions strewn about, stacks of fabric bolts tossed about, and the floor littered with the meager treasures of the seamstresses. Near the center of the room, she spied the chest that had held Austa's belongings emptied on the floor.

Austa was gone. Hope that the elder had managed to escape had filled Anippe's mind, but the knowledge that death had found the seamstress dashed away that fragile light.

Icy shivers filled Anippe. The small basket still clutched in her hands fell to the ground, her fingers too weak to hold it. With chattering teeth, she gathered up what few morsels of food that were about, cramming them into her mouth to quiet the babe. Loathe to touch the jewels, she stepped back. Then thoughts of survival crept in. She would need their value if she had any hopes of escape.

Plucking a small square of fabric from a basket of samples, she spread the blue silk on the top of a chest and bent to gather up what was there. The scrap of fabric soon held a small mound that included a brooch, a pair of jeweled comb, two rings, and a tiny fistful of clay coins. Removing the bundle strapped to her thigh, she tied all together as one except for the ram's head and the coins. Then she gathered the corners of the fabric and once again strapped the square to her thigh. The ram's head and coins were consigned to a smaller bundle fastened to a short length of cord and hung around her neck, falling between her breasts. It was small enough to resemble the good luck tokens many wore.

Her body trembling with fatigue, Anippe finally retreated to a far corner of the room where several of the stacked baskets formed a make-shift hiding place. She quickly began to pull bolts of fabric to the floor, unrolling them until a small mountain lie around her. Then into the center of this nest she crawled, covering herself with the beautiful fabrics Austa had coveted and protected. Warmth crept into Ankh and she curled into a ball and slept.

* * *

"Why wasn't this room closed?"

Anippe's eyes flew open, the hard voice of Loust seeming to shout directly into her ears.

"Look at this fine mess!"

Anippe held her breath as the slap of bare feet on the stone floor moved in her direction. Someone lifted the edge of her haven.

"What are you doing? The Master Tailor will be here on the morrow." Loust said. The tall staff he had been carrying the previous day beating against the floor. "Leave this for him to inventory. Just close the doors and post a guard until we are through."

Sweat beaded on Anippe's chest and wet the nape of her neck. The doors banged shut. If there were a guard outside, she would have to remain hidden until he left because like most of the doors in the Palace, they were not solid, but filled with artfully carved openings that allowed air to pass.

At dusk she crept out on hands and knees, crossing the center aisle to the balcony. Here the doors were thrown wide open. She stayed inside until the darkness was full and consumed her last crust of bread. No lanterns lit the courtyard. No balcony light shone, warm and inviting. Leaving there, she moved to the corridor door. There was no shadow of a guard on the other side, and as she listened holding her breath, no sound of anyone either.

Tugging on the door, Anippe found it opened easily, but where other than the busy main corridor was there to go.

Not knowing what she would find if she ventured further kept her a prisoner. Even the hidden staircase that led to the slaves alleys could hold danger. Returning to her nest, she waited for the coming day.

CHAPTER 16

Dawn brought the tramping of many feet, hurried along by the crack of a short whip.

"It is the order of Pharaoh that all shall be in readiness for the Royal family in two days. Move or you too shall burn on the pyre of the pretender." Bellowed a harsh voice.

Anippe crawled to the balcony. At the end of the far gardens near the river, she could see a rising cloud of black smoke. The acrid plumes rose to the sky, carrying the essence of the Prince of Egypt and his family to the gods. Unfortunately, the prevailing winds that day were unkind. Perhaps the gods were offended by the injustice which had occurred and using the breeze made their displeasure known. The stench wafted back to the Palace, stinging noses and tearing eyes.

Outside the carved doorway, a scraggly line of slaves moved through the hall. Those exiting carried stained fabrics or broken furniture, but nothing of value. All walked with downcast eyes that jerked from side to side, their fear evident. There were some she recognized vaguely from her days within their ranks. It was clear the butchering had befallen only the family of Pharaoh and those who knew them most intimately. The remainder, those who maintained the great palace, had been left to serve it still. She joined the line but instead of turning into the Queen's private chambers; moved towards the narrow cavern that encased the slaves' entrance.

Maybe she could escape the palace to find someone in the city who would help her. The alley, normally busy, was empty. Her steps echoed a warning. At the archway on the edge of freedom, she was halted abruptly.

"Go back, girl. No one is to leave save through the main hall."

Two guards, swords in hand, blocked her way. At the order to halt, other guards appeared in each doorway. Meekly, Anippe bowed her head, walking in the middle of the wide corridor until she approached the central staircase. Barely half-way down the long winding path of steps, she faltered. Weakness overcame her. Dizzy, unable to breathe past the fabric once again tied across her face, she stumbled. The clattering approach of slaves bearing great vats of boiling water and lye made no impression as she sat slumped on the steps, head in hands.

Through eyes brimming with tears, she saw a slender set of legs pause before her. A young girl crouched down, shaking Anippe's shoulder urgently.

"Get up quickly," the girl coaxed, "before someone sees you."

Miserable, Anippe knew she had to move, but her shaking knees would not carry her. She gagged against the cloth. Deftly, it was plucked from her face.

"You will not need that here." The rag was dipped in the water and lye mix then shoved back into her hand. "Just start scrubbing while you rest. I am Nisbet, just stay with me." Reaching , she ran her hand over Anippe's swollen belly. "I don't remember a woman with child here." Inquisitive eyes looked long into hers and then moved to study her face. With the gag gone, the new girl saw a face familiar but out of place among the slaves directed to scrub away the stain of the previous regency. Her eyes narrowed.

"What is your name?" queried the helpful one slowly, barely more than a child herself.

"Anippe."

There was a brief pause. Anippe heard the gulping breath Nisbet swallowed. The girl knew, and suddenly she was afraid. It was evident to Anippe as the fingers touching her arm turned to ice in a single heartbeat.

"Mistress." The girl sat back on her heels, the shocked whisper a hiss of acknowledgment, then only slightly louder, "Father, Father help me." She called without taking her eyes off Anippe's face.

A stooped man crept over on hands and knees. "What are you doing?" He demanded, darting quick glances over his shoulder.

At the end of the long corridor, a bell rang, catching the guards' attention. The few guards who had spent the time talking among themselves and ignoring the slaves moved to the lower hall. There, an old woman offered the guards a refreshment to relieve their toils. The slaves received nothing, but their busy hands worked at an even more feverish pace as the guards filed by.

As soon as the last javelin-toting man walked past, Anippe's two partners put their heads together. Urgent whispers passed between them. Finally, the old man raised his head, peering intently at Anippe, who was trying to follow Nisbet's direction. When he looked back at the young slave girl, she nodded her head in affirmation.

"We go there." He directed, pointing to the inside wall with its thirty-foot statues of Isis and Ra. Between the two gods was a massive carved lion.

Anippe shook her head. She wanted to go out of the Palace instead of towards the inside, but as the elder dragged his bucket and scuttled sideways, she followed. The returning guards eyed the great hall with no acknowledgment of any difference in the placement of the workers.

At the lion's foot, the man put Anippe behind him,

pushing her closer to the wall. The great foot extended sideways five feet into the corridor, leaving a narrow space between it and the wall.

"Crawl behind," he muttered. "There is a doorway. Stay there. Be quiet."

His daughter, returning with a full bucket, searched for the man. With a nod, he returned to his work, indicating she should as well.

CHAPTER 17

Anippe crouched behind the stone lion's foot. The opening was narrow. Stone scratched at her from both sides as she crawled backwards. Where the leg extended up in what appeared a shadow in the cleft of the carving, she found a low doorway. The dim light showed the outline of a staircase that climbed steeply upwards inside the structure. The passage grew darker as the steps ascended. Sitting on the bottom-most step, Anippe waited. The hours grew long. She was hungry and uncomfortable.

What could be worse than this uncertain future? she wondered.

The staircase was so small she could touch both walls at the same time. Her bare feet slid along the stone; the way was steep but, once she started, she did not turn back.

Eventually, she could see a slice of bright light above her.

On the last step, she looked with amazement at a hidden corridor. To her right was solid stone, but five feet away a carved facade of light wood allowed light to shine in. She found an ornate stool near the facade. Approaching it, she caught her breath. She was high above the harem rooms. In this hidden place, she could see below the slaves that scoured the marble floors. The tailor ran from divan to divan, tripping in his haste. Behind him, slaves ripped the damask away to reveal the lamb's wool padding beneath. She watched with interest as the fat, once insolent man pulled at his hair.

"Take it away," he screamed at the slaves. A piece stained beyond repair was carried out. One that withstood his inspection was carefully stripped of the remaining shreds by one set of slaves, even as another set cut new damask to cover it. Loust walked among the workers. His presence frightened them to even greater speed. Watching in fascination at the whirling sandstorm of activity, Anippe sat on the stool, sure that as long as she was silent, no one would find her. There was humor in knowing that all the preening, all the *secret* struggles for power that occurred in the rooms below, were easily witnessed from here. Who had watched? Who knew?

Bored with the antics below, she walked along the winding corridor. The wall line followed the pattern of the great statues without a point she had never considered before, ending abruptly above the baths. There were still several feet before the outside wall of the room below. It was curious that the corridor ended short of the farthest edge. While she considered this phenomenon, she brushed a hand across the stone. It was different from the rest. The shading was darker, the texture not as smooth. There were also stones jutting out at odd intervals. One, she noted when she touched its surface, looked dirtier than the rest.

The stone felt wobbly at her touch. Anippe put her hand on it, pushing lightly. The stone moved. She pushed harder. The stone wall swiveled on a silent base. Now she found a circular staircase leading once more overhead into darkness. She climbed.

This much smaller overview was of the Queen's chambers. It crossed the room along the wall between her private bedroom and the main room. There was another stool. Here, because of the light from both sides, Anippe felt exposed, sure she could be seen if she was not careful. She crawled back down the staircase, pushing the wall shut. Curled in a corner, she waited, napping without dreams.

A hand touching hers woke her late in the evening. Now the hidden corridor was lit by the artificial light of flickering oil lamps that were within the harem but passed through the lattice wall. Resting against the wall, the old man offered a hard crust of bread along with a bowl of water.

"Tell me," he said when she was through, "tell me your tale. For if it matches that which my daughter has spoken of, I will help you. But if it does not, I will not endanger my only child or myself."

Anippe spoke of her life first as the old man's daughter would have known, a new woman brought into the harem of Pharaoh already with child. A woman who kept separate from the others. Then she spoke of her life before as a free man, of Austa and Kaakhsi, then of the Queen's offer to save the child. While she spoke, the sounds of rebuilding below them continued. She heard the occasional crack of the short whip, followed by a yelp of pain. A long silence followed her story. The lantern sputtered. She could barely discern man from the wall.

"It is as my girl said. Often while she worked in the Queen's bath, the Queen would converse with the Panhsjet, the great black witch. My girl heard this tale from them. They believe all others are deaf and dumb." Rising with a tired sigh, he continued. "Tonight, they finish making ready for the new Queen. Tomorrow she will arrive. Then I will come for you. You must listen and heed quickly, mistress, to save your life."

When he moved to leave, Anippe stopped him. "How did you know of this place?"

"My whole life I have spent sweeping the Great Hall. I am its keeper. Often, I would see Pharaoh, then by the grace of the gods, he would disappear. It frightened me. One day I saw him near the great stone Ra. Before I could turn away, he stepped behind. He was gone for a long while. When at last he returned, I allowed curiosity to guide my steps. I found the door and the staircase."

"Have you been to the end?"

"It ends at the far wall."

Anippe kept her knowledge to herself. "Who else knows of this place? Is it safe to stay here?"

"I do not think anyone else knows. This was built when Pharaoh's father was a small child. I do not think Pharaoh even told his brother, for I have never seen him here and it is said he is of many perversions. There may be others who know, but I have never seen them."

When he left, she crawled to the opposite wall, peeking through one of the openings. Below her, all was near readiness. Slaves on tall ladders hung new sheer draperies. The tailor was gone, the alabaster shone, and incense burned heavily to cleanse the air. The large rooms looked surprisingly empty. It seemed that, without the harem, there was not really much there.

CHAPTER 18

A dry hand brought Anippe from a place where shadowy figures chased her across the smooth silk of polished marble. She was very hungry and hard to rouse. She opened her mouth to quarrel at his command, but he took her hand in his dry one and pulled her gently to her feet.

"Now, child. Pharaoh's Queen arrives. There is much confusion."

For a moment, hope rose. The old man hesitated near the bottom of the steps. "If you are asked, your Pharaoh is Manu. Do not forget, or it will cost you your life."

Those lining the Great Hall, faces pressed against the stone in allegiance, did not notice three more crowded against the wall. The revered statue of Ra was not a place for one's dirty feet to touch. Anippe realized this was why no one found the doorway behind the curved foot. The kneeling people stayed a good distance away. She also noticed that the people who surrounded her all bore a new tattoo. The black beak of a hawk burned above the tattoo that said 'slave.' This tattoo not only identified the bearer as property, and to whom they belonged.

Following behind, she crawled along the wall towards the slaves' corridor. While drums beat and whistles blew a shrill tune, the First Wife of Manu Pharaoh of Egypt was carried for the first time to the Queen's chamber. She was obese to the point her sedan chair was specially made. Unable to walk the distance on her own power, she indolently accepted the homage of people whose fear for their very lives dictated their behavior.

Behind the Queen, the wives of Pharaoh followed, not in the orderly manner of his brother's women, but loud and garish, each vying to be first. Through her lashes, Anippe saw evidence of much abuse on these women whose sheer garments left them virtually naked. Long scratches and bruises from pinching or perhaps biting were evident. It seemed the wives of Manu were as brutal as their lord.

Their way out was similarly arduous, blocked by slaves carrying boxes, chests, pieces of furniture that the new inhabitants had brought with them. Anippe marveled at the height of hysteria in the movements of others. Perhaps it would abate when the women were settled. In the courtyard, the old man joined a crowd headed away from the Palace. These, the people who had worked through the night, were headed for their beds. They stopped at a community pot for a bowl of rice and millet gruel. Anippe barely chewed the mealy offering and sighed sadly when it was gone. The old man handed her his bowl. Nisat joined them. They moved towards the dormitories, speaking in low tones.

"How do you know all that you do?" Anippe asked Nisat. She understood how the old man, through the years, would have discerned what he had, but how did this young girl do so?

"The Queen's women are tongueless and, if I am not incorrect, sleep, eat, and live within the walls of her quarters. She does not, did not share well."

Anippe swallowed hard, realizing her error.

"No," said Nisat, her voice was a giggling bell. "But I was not one of her women. I was merely the running legs for the women who spent hours every day scraping and oiling the temple that was her earthly body. Even with the new Queen, I take away and fetch and, when I am not running, I sit against the wall waiting. I hear because I am nothing, I am unseen."

Anippe nodded to her young savior. She did not touch the girl, because earlier when Anippe had laid her hand on Nisat's arm; the girl had crumbled to the floor, head bowed in submission. Anippe did not enjoy that power and it would surely raise questions.

Three stories tall, the dormitories were built to be utilitarian, not necessarily comfortable. Nisat led the way to the top floor of the woman's building. There, at the top of the building where the sun baked the roof, and the air was too hot to breathe. The dormitory clerk would not easily find Anippe.

"I have to go back." Nisat explained. "My place is in the Queen's bath. Stay here until I return for you." When Anippe stared at the still raw tattoo, Nisat touched it self-consciously. "If you are asked, your lord is Manu," she mumbled before she ran down the steps.

* * *

Anippe spent the first day waiting in the stuffy silence until Nisat returned. They then washed at the community fountain and ate. On the second day, Anippe was plagued with an over-full bladder. Unable to wait any longer, she left her hiding place and carefully made her way to the room on the first floor where she could use the cess-pots. Returning to the dormitory room, she passed the doorway leading to the tunic room. Sighing with relief, she removed her filthy tunic, which now was tightly stretched across her bulging stomach. A fresh, larger tunic felt delightfully extravagant. Her euphoria was short-lived.

"Ho. What are you doing here, lazy girl? Why aren't you in your place?" The crone who oversaw the dormitory stood in the doorway. "Get out. Get out. Go before I take my staff to your back."

Anippe hurried away. She was sure she could outpace the old woman, but there was no need to bring attention to herself. Once in the courtyard, she stopped to think. She did not dare go back to the Palace. She needed to be free of this place. Following a pathway to the left which would eventually lead to one of the lesser gates, she tried to think of a plan. Would there be guards? Would they just let her leave? She was sure not.

At one gateway, she paused. Guards questioned some that appeared to be gardeners. The question was simple "Who is your Pharaoh?" When the answer was not swift in return, a blade slashed, a head rolled. Stuffing her fist in her mouth, she hurried past. Before her was a cart full of those who had not given their answers in a timely manner. The cart approached the gate, pulling to one side as an empty cart entered. Tilted back with the weight of the bodies dragging from the back, the front end lifted past the rump of the donkey that pulled it and blocked the lead man's view. Eyes with no vision gazed upward at the buzzards that circled. A thin stream of blood followed. Heads lay akimbo to bodies no longer attached. Anippe's stomach rose, but her fear of the new palace residents surpassed that. The lead man made a clucking sound, and the cart jerked back into motion. There was no time for thought.

Anippe threw herself among the still warm bodies, asking the gods for forgiveness.

Barely pausing at the gate, the cart rolled out, headed to the river. When they were out of sight of the gate, Anippe slid off. She did not notice the woman who looked up just in time to see one of the dead rise and faint where she stood.

CHAPTER 19

For two days, Anippe fared by begging and sleeping in doorways at the far ends of the smallest side streets. It was not enough. She was starving and too often running in fear from the soldiers who routinely patrolled the marketplace. With no idea where to go and no family to go to, she was destitute. Her tunic bespoke the House of Pharaoh and many eyes watched her.

"Get out, whore. Go back to your man," screamed the fruit seller after Anippe had asked for food. "Maybe he'll beat that bastard out of you." Then he chased her away.

Not all the occupants of the marketplace were honest merchants. This was another world Anippe knew nothing about. That world, however, knew her. Not as the mother of the true Pharaoh, but as a lost girl who could be used for their benefit. Since her confused arrival, a ragged pair had stalked her, watching while one after another of her crude attempts at begging were turned aside. Here she received a crust of bread, maybe a rind of melon, but she fared poorly and her strength was ebbing. Even in the night, when the honest merchants went home and the dark traders came out, they watched. Soon she would be more open to their advance.

In an alleyway, Anippe leaned exhausted against a crumbling wall, tears failing her.

From their vantage point, the pair, a man and a woman, watched. "She is far with child," pointed out the man.

"But look how fair of face she is," the woman said with a sigh.

"How can you see through all that dirt?" he scoffed.

"She's not as dirty as you," she retorted.

For another hour, they sat. The girl did not move. Finally, the woman grunted to her feet. "I'll go to her. Stay here until I signal. But..." she turned, wagging her finger, "be ready. Do not wander off."

Moving in a haphazard manner that added to her

beggar's demeanor, the woman crossed the open space. When she was close to Anippe, she squatted. The girl made no move to leave or offered any sign she had even noticed the other. "Poor babe," the woman crooned, softly touching Anippe's sunburned arm. The younger girl jolted awake. "No, no, lamb. I did not mean to startle you, nor do I wish to harm you." Removing her hand, she waited until the haunted look left Anippe's eyes and fatigue returned. From within her robe, she pulled a half loaf of soft, fresh bread. "I have not much, but I would share this with you," she offered, tearing off a small piece.

At another time, Anippe would have wondered how one so wretchedly poor and dirty could have so tempting a morsel; today the pregnant mother did not care. Anippe reached for the torn piece.

The hag pulled it back, giving instead the larger piece of loaf. "I am old. You, child, are in greater need. The ascension this day of Manu, Pharaoh of Egypt, to immortality has made many generous." The woman watched Anippe eat, interrupting only at those moments when she believed the younger would choke. Squeezing the flesh on Anippe's upper arm, she noted it was slow to rebound. Not only was the girl badly sunburned, but she was dehydrated as well. This was not good for the hag's plans. The sun would kill without mercy. "Stay here, eat slowly. I am going to get you water." At the fountain, she filled her beggar's bowl.

With her hunger momentarily sated by bread, and two bowls of water, Anippe rested. Offering her good Samaritan an embarrassed smile, she murmured, "Thank you. I have not found as generous a sponsor as yours."

"Tut, child. I have been here for a long, long time. I am, as is the desert dust that blows around for all time." From within a hidden pocket, she pulled a small jar of salve. The jar was cracked and stoppered with a piece of rag, but the salve the hag rubbed onto Anippe's exposed flesh cooled the bright red burn.

"Are you a physician?"

The woman cackled in laughter., "A physician? Oh no, I am as you are. One who has lost hope and faith. One of the fallen." She waited; no response came. "This tunic you wear is slave garb, yet you have no tattoo."

"I am not a slave," was the whispered answer.

"But you are alone. You are begging and soon to birth."
Still, no explanation came. Sitting cross-legged before the girl,
the hag breathed close to Anippe's face, foul breath hinged
with truth. "Your man is dead." Pause. "He did not recognize
his new master quick enough."

A single tear rolled down Anippe's cheek, gliding over
the salve as water from the Nile ran from the oars of the heavy
barges.

"You cannot stay here. You will not be safe." Rising to
her feet with difficulty, the hag tugged at her. "Come with me."
Anippe looked at her with alarm. "There is a place where the
poor and homeless go when darkness falls. You are not the
only one without. But to stay here means to put yourself in the
way of the night guards. I don't know how long you have been
here but, if they have not found you, you are very lucky
indeed. Many are rogue, foul. They will consider you an object
to use, to share, to discard."

The woman's words frightened Anippe, who looked

about in fear. Though the sun still shone, she could see the guards with their long-spiked javelins. A few ragged beggars moved past them as if a sign. Timidly, she allowed the tugging hand to lead her on.

CHAPTER 20

"Most of the beggars leave the marketplace when it closes,"

said the woman. "I am Baet, and what I say is true. Pharaoh's

curfew is strict. At night, only prostitutes and those that deal

with them mix with the black-market merchants of drugs and

other illegal or stolen goods. Their customers move freely

among them, for each pays a high tithe for the soldiers to look

away. There are pick-pockets, cut-purses, and thieves who are

safe, but beggars are vermin easily disposed of and never

missed. The marketplace is a complicated and dangerous place

to be when the sun travels to its rest."

Anippe's protector led the way from street to alley to

narrow pathway. On the outskirts of the city, far from the

marketplace, was a temporarily abandoned work site. It was

part of the elaborate aqueduct system and still being built when an untimely death of several priests who were members of an old cult, the Eridinii, had halted construction. It was said that even though the two workers involved were sacrificed, disemboweled while their screams rose above the site, the priests still wandered through the area. Even after the High Priest came to cleanse and bless the area, no workers would return. Freeman or slave, taskmaster or guard, none would set foot here.

While the emissaries of Pharaoh pondered the issue, and in the absence of any workman, the all-seeing and vigilant network of beggars set up their puny squatters' village. They were not afraid of the dead, for the afterlife could be no worse than what they faced daily. Baet and her man, Menes, considered by the others of their community to be cold hearted and cruel, ruled. For many years, they had prayed on the very weak among the other beggars, threatened any stronger, and eliminated those who would compete for power. They had claimed rights to the open end of the duct system. This was the place Baet led Anippe.

Shortly after they arrived, Menes returned. He also

expressed concern for the poor, bereft girl. Leaving quickly, he brought back an armful of fairly fresh straw and a coarse blanket for her to sleep on.

"Thank you." Anippe smiled, unaware that he had stolen these goods from another. Though she did not know what tomorrow would bring, for now she was safe.

CHAPTER 21

Anippe's sense of security would have been dashed had she been aware of what she left behind within the Palace walls. It is said only the masters do not know of the power of their slaves. So was it within Pharaoh's walls. Where Rakhenemet had been beloved. His brother was not. Though men swore allegiance to Manu, they did so only to endure until revenge was achieved.

One of these men was Nefersi, father of Nisat. When his daughter came running to him with the news Anippe was missing and a search of the dormitory had not unearthed her, he wasted no time. The dormitory keeper admitted to driving Anippe out, but no one remembered seeing where she went. Nefersi, born free but sold cunningly into slavery, had a large and extensive family beyond the stone walls. They included men of value, merchants, and even a high-ranking Priest. His place in the Queen's Palace had always borne fruit of knowledge the disciples of Egypt had used. Now he made it known to his people this girl was missing from the palace and she needed to be found. He did not tell all he knew of her for there was always the chance of espionage, but he did not search alone.

Days passed, then one merchant told another the story of a peasant who had fainted when she witnessed one of the dead rise out of a cart full of corpses and walk away. A woman heavy with child, possibly that of the Lord of the Dead. It had happened on the day after the new Queen moved into her palace. The merchant hoped it was not a bad omen. These same two men repeated this conversation in several common places within the palace gates, speaking openly in the presence of slaves but carefully avoiding the guards.

Eventually, the tale traveled to Nefersi. The search moved outside the stone walls.

CHAPTER 22

Though she knew little of pregnancy, Anippe was sure her time was almost over. Ungainly and uncomfortable, she rarely left the area surrounding the aqueduct. Baet made it clear she wanted to help, stating it was not safe for the girl to go far. Even Menes doted on Anippe with fatherly attention. Anippe, grateful for their loving attention, paid heed to their advice, just as she would have the parents she barely remember.

On this day, however, the sun's relentless heat was subdued, yet she was curiously unsettled. By mid-morn, she cast away all semblance of docility, walking back along the narrow path. In the marketplace, her feeling of unease grew. Moving through the crowd, she finally saw Baet ahead, leaning on a fruit stand. She was almost at the elder's elbow when a voice called through the bickering noise.

"Anippe. Anippe."

Both she and Baet turned at the same time. She saw Nisat, who had been shopping for supplies to mix her bath salts, smiling in joy. Baet saw the sudden ending of her darker plans. Roughly, she grabbed the pregnant girl, pulling her back between the booths. Menes dropped the fruit he was pilfering to throw himself up as a barrier, stopping Nisat's advance.

"No!" Anippe fought to free herself. "I know her. She is a friend."

Baet hung on. "She wears Pharaoh's garb. There are no friends there. Only those who would separate you from your child." Baet was no fool. She had carefully watched Anippe until she knew where control would lie.

"What?" Anippe stopped struggling.

"Listen, I told you, I was as you are. When you are a lone woman and you birth a child, it is taken from you to be thrown into the Nile."

"No," Anippe gasped, her knees buckling beneath her.

"Yes. It is true." Baet's face softened. "I wanted to spare you. Hide you, keep you safe. My precious girl, you can trust no one who wears Pharaoh's tattoo." The shaking girl became pliable once more. "This way. I know a way to get through where we won't be seen. This way."

They moved quickly. Somewhere along the way, bands of pain tightened around Anippe's belly. She could not draw a breath until the pain passed. Though they were infrequent, Baet told her they would increase. The child was coming.

In the dark night, Baet sent Menes for a midwife. Among the homeless, there were several. The three sat around the fire in the open, not far from where Anippe lay.

"How much longer?" Menes complained.

"A while yet," said the midwife. "She is sleeping, but the pains will wake her soon."

Baet sat, happily humming, "I think, Menes, it is time for you to prepare the new mother for the happy news."

"Shouldn't we wait to make sure it's a boy?" he asked.

"No, she will be glad for either. A girl now will mean a boy later. It won't matter."

After he moved off, the midwife turned her shrewish eyes to Baet. "What is your plan, Baet?"

"Why would I tell you? You might thwart me."

"Ha. As if I could. Me and you, we have been here a long, long time. If you didn't trust me, you wouldn't have sent for me. There are others, younger, stronger."

"Well," said Baet, so pleased she couldn't stop wiggling. "We found this girl loose in the marketplace, probably turned out because the mistress didn't want the brat so close. Or the old fool died, and the mistress saw fit to put out the trash with her coming child. It doesn't much matter for I have another customer who wishes to keep her comfortable place, but her husband is demanding a child. This cosseted bitch does not want to ruin her body. She has kept him at bay for months because he believes she is with child, and is not smart enough to figure it out. She'll buy the brat at a healthy sum, then I'll cut out the girl's tongue and sell her at a slave auction. I'll be rid of them both and have a hefty purse besides."

"Would it be easier if I let the girl die?" asked the midwife.

"What, you fool. Who will nurse the babe? I will not

turn it over until I have my money. If it takes three or four days, how will I take care of the child? And I would lose my slave fee. I think not."

Together, the wicked two cackled in merriment. Lying on her bed of straw, Anippe pressed her eyes tightly together. She had heard all. Even here, she was not safe.

At dawn, the child came. A boy, small and wailing. He nursed fitfully while she tried to clean him with the edge of the blanket. The midwife left after the birthing, unconcerned both mother and babe were filthy, and the new mother was unsure.

When Anippe asked for water, Baet brought an old basin full of catch water. Though it was fresh, it was not clean. The girl did the best she could with it for both herself and the boy. Exhausted, she lay with him in her arms. Her last sight before sleep was Menes approaching the fire pit.

When Anippe woke, Baet had much food for her to eat. There were also several urns of clear water, a clean robe for herself and swaddling for the infant. She was never to know that in this Menes had asserted himself. He had known a wife and children of his own at one time. He knew what would be needed to keep death from finding this new little family.

CHAPTER 23

Baet lay snoring near the fire when Anippe rose again, sore but determined.

"Huh. Where are you going?" slurred the old woman. Menes had also brought a jug to celebrate their soon to be riches. He was senseless across the fire.

"I am only going to relieve myself," demurred Anippe. "Maybe to walk with the baby for a few moments to lull him back to sleep." Baet watched her suspiciously. "You have been so good to us, Baet. I am so thankful. We, you and I, will have to think of a good name for our little baby. You and I. Tomorrow."

Smiling, the old woman laid back down. "Tomorrow," she repeated before the snoring returned louder than before.

Moving in an indirect path, sure she could trust no one, Anippe gained the outer rim of the site and began stealthily moving back towards the city. When she passed the place

where she had buried the two small pouches of trinkets,

keeping the secret even from Baet, she unearthed them,

strapping one on to her inner thigh and allowing the other to

dangle again between her breasts.

The fear of night guards haunted her steps, slowing her,

but dawn found her past the marketplace and once more at the

Palace gates. Searching the line of freeman and merchants

waiting for entry, she finally found a face she recognized. A

strong woman who worked in the Queen's Palace. A

soothsayer whose loud voice and commanding physic

frightened her listeners into believing.

"Please, mistress," said Anippe, bowing her head as she

approached the woman. From her tiny bag of trinkets, she

produced a small ring. "I know you go to do the gods' business

for the Queen; would you deliver a message for me to my sister

who is there?"

"Move away," the woman ordered.

Anippe held up the ring. When she had the soothsayer's

attention, she spoke again, "I know I can trust you, that the

Queen trusts you, that you have brought your wisdom here for a long while."

The woman looked nervously around, but greed and pride kept her from moving away.

Anippe lowered her voice. "My sister and I have been separated, perhaps for the rest of our lives. I want her only to know that I have born a son. She works for the Queen only, in the baths. She is the mixer of potions and oils. There is no need for you to bring me further information. I will wait here until you have told her. I will know." Pressing the coin into the woman's hand just as the gate swung open, she stepped back under a scraggly olive tree.

It was her hope Nisat would understand but not be endangered. Anippe once again had no place to go. Her only hope was a woman who glowed at the sight of a coin.

The soothsayer proved that day why she served the previous Queen and this Queen as well. Where Neferet had been the epitome of decorum, her successor lived for theatrics. Working herself into a frenzy, the soothsayer threw herself around the bathing room while the new royalty was steamed, scraped, and oiled. In a high-pitched wail, she screeched predictions about common peoples' sacrifices to the new monarch. In the middle of her tirade, she stated twice that the sister to one of the Queen's slaves had born a son who would grow to dedicate his life to the throne of Egypt.

The Queen paid this no mind.

A slave girl took notice. The girl approached the soothsayer as she left, offering a flask of enticingly scented salts, asking only where last this sister had been seen. When the tall woman left, Nisat ran, skidding down the staircase.

Within minutes, the old man who had not been out of the Palace in years peered around the edge of the gate. There was, indeed, a woman seated under the olive tree, a tiny bundle resting on her lap. While another member of his Eridinii occupied the guard, the old slave slipped out of the gate. Casually, he squatted near the girl. When she opened her mouth to speak, he held up his hand.

"I do not wish to know; it is only good that you are safe. My people devised a plan to take you from the city to a place you will be safe. You will not see me again, nor Nisat. In a moment, a man will leave here who wears a blue corded belt

with silver tassels. Follow him. He will take you to safety."

"I cannot go near the marketplace," she whispered.

"You will not."

When the short, rotund man strolled through the gates,

Anippe fell in step behind him. He led her down a side street

not far from the Palace walls. Once inside the nondescript

house, she was offered nourishment and a place to sleep. She

was told that, in a few days' time, she would be taken far from

there. No further information was provided.

CHAPTER 24

Soft eyes of liquid brown, long trembling lashes. Anippe had never been so close to a camel before and she found the creature beautiful. The camel's fur was just a shade creamier than white. She was docile, meek, seductive, and shy. The tradesman sat astride a much larger camel of dark brown whose haughty expression brooked no interference. Her new friends had brought her here and placed her in this man's hands. He had been promised gold when she was delivered with her squalling brat intact. As long as she did not slow down their progress, there would be no problem. The time for this journey to start had come.

For several hours, the tradesman and his men had worked to tie great loads on the camels. From here to there, they plied their trade. A rich load of spices and fabrics had come to this city; now goods of the land would go to another. The girl was merely part of the load. A young eunuch sat among the camels as they sang their lullaby. An old slave, toothless and bowlegged, ran about, checking cinches and halters. At a grunted command from his master, he approached Anippe. He showed her how to mount the beast, where to balance her seat and hold on.

"Do not worry, young mistress," he said with a smile. "Tutu will be very good." Affectionately, he patted the camel. "She has been well trained since birth. I know. I trained her myself. And she is tethered front and back to the rest of the caravan. Now all you have to do is stay on."

The caravan moved ahead towards the Western gate. Their progress was slow but steady. When at last the gate was in view, they all stopped. Before them was a great crowd waiting to leave. The gates were open. Why didn't they go? When the old slave moved back down the line towards the rear, Anippe stopped him. "Why do we wait?"

"There is a group of Egyptians entering and they have the first right," he replied with a sneer.

"But we are so far away from the gate. Others are much closer."

Indeed, other caravans seemed to be jammed one into the other. The tradesmen waited patiently.

"Yes." The camel handler's wide smile loomed up at her. "But when the waiting is done, they will still be waiting."

Anippe could not stop the smile she passed back. "And you know this for certain?"

"Look about you." His arms swept over the area. "Do you see the men who stand about us? Did you notice that while we sweat to load the beasts, they do not help? No one enters or leaves the city without paying passage among the handlers. There are many and they all have their own packs, as do jackals. Ackwodoh uses the same handler every time he comes to this city. They allow him to enter and to leave. They also keep his self and his goods safe while he is here," said the handler. "Ackwodoh may be last in line, but he will be first to leave."

Anippe looked up the line, then back at him with a question.

"If you are not Egyptian, you must be outside the gates by dark. Ackwodoh is not Egyptian, and the sun falls quickly. Others will be forced to stop and negotiate the price of passage. We will just be taken out and released." Again, his smile widened.

"How do you know this old man? What makes you think your lord is special and he will pass without payment?"

Laughing loudly as he clamored to his seat above a camel's load, he called back. "Because Ackwodoh took the handlers pock-marked sister to wife."

"Hut. Hut," shouted the handlers. The camels moved forward; a passage opened as they approached. By the time they went through the gates, they were trotting; at the bottom of sand ramp they were fairly running. Anippe held on for dear life; she did not yet trust her wooden saddle. The baby was strapped securely across her breast. Within her head, a voice asked; Are you afraid? She looked out over the desert towards her future. Aloud she answered, "No."

CHAPTER 25

They traveled for six days, taking only brief rests. The camels

seemed to be able to go on forever, through the heat of day and

the cold of night. Anippe learned to sleep in the saddle, lulled

by the men who sang for the camels. She was given meager

amounts of water and some dried meat. She feared the meat

had been a camel that had not been able to keep up the pace.

They stopped only once during the day. The wind had risen

and great clouds of dust swept towards them. All the camels

knelt. The men cowered beside them, covered by their robes

and choking for air. The old man huddled with Anippe,

protecting the baby. It was not unusual; he told her, for the

wind to suck an infant's breath away and leave it dead. He

frightened her.

When she believed her bones could stand no more, a

shout and a pointing arm showed the way to a small green space on the horizon. An oasis. It grew ever larger until they stood at its edge. Sheep drank from the spillage of a low spring-fed well and the camels waited. Anippe wanted nothing other than to climb off the camel and submerge her face in the cool water. How could she have believed this animal was a great cuddly pet? A child offered water to the men at the well. When it came to be Anippe's turn to be handed the cup, Ackwodah moved towards her. With a firm grip on her arm, he pulled her further into the oasis.

Amid the palms and fronds, Anippe was surprised to see large colorful tents. They were made of long woven pieces of wool. Each section boasted an intricate pattern in the weave. There were sheep and children everywhere. Pointing to the ground, Ackwodah left her behind as he was ushered into the largest of the tents. A breeze shuddered the fronds and drifted over her. Dirty and uncertain, Anippe did not sit but stood where she had been left. Women circled her, shrewd eyes taking in her obviously Egyptian features. Those men who wandered past leered, talking in a tongue she did not understand. At last, she was beckoned into the tent. Ackwodah sat on a mat near the headman. He balanced a small jingling pouch happily on his knee.

"This is where you will stay. This is where I was told to bring you." Grunting, he climbed to his feet. "I don't know if they will understand you or you them. That is not my problem." So, he left her.

The headman sat in silence until a child ran in and whispered in his ear. He gave a command to a young girl kneeling near the entrance and she left.

"Sit."

The command startled Anippe. She was not sure if it was the sudden sound of his voice or that she was able to understand his words.

"I am Ahab-ram. You are now part of my family. Do not look so angry. You are not a slave, or wife, or even concubine, merely part of my family. No one will question it. You have been sent here to be safe, but you are tired and we will talk of this later." A woman entered, followed by several adolescent girls. "This is Shareefa. She is my wife. My light.

There are few here who speak your tongue, but you will learn ours. Shareefa will guide you." Giving several abrupt orders in a language that seemed to roll all words into one, he left the tent.

Shareefa came to stand before Anippe. She did not speak, but eyed the other woman openly. Unlike the long robe worn by the others, Shareefa wore billowing pants of a sheer fabric with a jewel encrusted girdle. Her silken halter was heavily embroidered with sparkling gems worked into the stitches. Her feet and long neck were bare, but many bangles jangled far up her forearm from the wrist. While they stood facing, more women entered the tent. Shareefa turned to motion the ones who crept closer away and Anippe saw the thick, black fall of hair down Shareefa's back. Not straight, but waving across her skin like the ripples on the desert sand. She pointed to herself, saying clearly, "Shareefa."

There was more babble that Anippe thought might be the dark-haired woman's title. When she was through, she pointed to Anippe who answered merely, "Anippe."

A heavily jeweled woman reached for Anippe, and

Shareefa slapped her away. The other went to the edge of the carpet, sulking.

"Anippe," repeated Shareefa, placing her hand on Anippe's chest. At the touch of her hand, the baby hidden in Anippe's robes cried out shrilly.

No longer could Shareefa control the women. They crowded closer, each talking at the same time. Inquiring fingers tore away at the dust-filled robes, exposing the tiny infant clutched in his mother's trembling arms. He struggled weakly, rooting about for her breast. There were tears in Anippe's eyes. She was so tired, so thirsty.

Shareefa became a whirlwind, shoving other women away, pinching them when they did not move fast enough. Not knowing what the other said or even caring, Anippe sunk to the mat and put the child to nurse. She watched Shareefa move about the tent. In the far corner, behind one of the transparent curtains, several sleeping mats were stacked. Dragging one away, she left it near the large raised platform. A few women returned with a large metal basin and several urns. Dull eyes watched the activity. Soon her son was done with his meager meal and dozed. Shareefa lifted him gently, handing him to a pudgy woman with round, rosy cheeks. Once separated from his mother, he was bathed, then wrapped in a clean cloth. The pudgy girl, who herself had an infant son, hid the tears sliding across her cheeks as she caressed his withered limbs. Only once did she look up to meet Shareefa's stare, silently shaking her head before she placed the sleeping baby in a woven basket.

Shareefa and the other woman worked their healing on Anippe. Stripping her, directing her to squat in the tub while they rubbed a scented liquid over her. They washed her head, rubbing at the slight bristle where hair should have grown. Once the bathing was through, there was food. Fruit, stewed meat, and thick milk. Laying on the pallet while Shareefa sat above her on the platform, Anippe thought she could hear music in the distance, but was not sure if she was only dreaming.

During the night, Anippe was awakened by the child's whimper. Reaching into the basket, she found it empty. Bolting upright, she encountered soft hands gently pushing her down.

In the lantern light was the pudgy girl; already the baby sucked hungrily at a strange breast. She whispered words that were not understood. Finally, she reached out to squeeze Anippe's dry breast, then took Anippe's hand to her own, round and full of life-giving milk. Laying back, Anippe watched. She would not let this woman steal away with the baby, but the gentle rocking and singing of the nursing mother lulled her back to dreamless sleep.

Waking early, as was her habit, Anippe looked over the room. Many mats had been spread while she had been sleeping. There were women and children all about her. In the basket, the baby slept, a little dribble of milk on his cheek. Over the side of the platform, two pairs of eyes watched. When they saw her looking back, they jumped up and moved away. The two little girls tumbled over Shareefa, who still dozed in the first light of day. She roused, laughing and tickling the toddlers. Calling out, she woke the rest of the occupants.

Anippe's babe was given to her to suckle for a short time before the other, called Adsheed, took him back. Shareefa dragged a sulking woman forward, indicating her to be

Samihah. They looked enough alike to be sisters. When Samihah balked at the rapid commands the older woman gave to her, Shareefa rapped her sharply beside the head, sending her tumbling. Sniffing audibly, Samihah took Anippe's hand and led her away.

Many of the women wore the same plain, unbleached garment Anippe had been given. It covered them from neck to ankles with sleeves to the mid-forearm. It merely slid over one's head and carried no adornment, though Shareefa and a few others wore a bright sash with long fringe. Anippe soon learned that this garb was worn during the working day or under the long bright robes of both men and women.

Once out of the tent, Samihah's tears dried magically. She showed Anippe to a small tent where she could relieve herself, a separate place to wash, and where there was food available. Later, she gave a short tour, saving for last the viewing of the herds of sheep. Proudly she stood, her arms pointing to the power of Ahab-ram. Born and raised in the city, Anippe was indeed impressed by the seemingly endless vista of woolly backs. Throughout it all, Samihah would point and give a word for Anippe to identify what she saw.

Learning from Samihah was difficult. The woman of nomads seemed to have no patience with the Egyptian. Anippe learned more from the children who followed her about, even when Samihah tried to chase them away. It was a few days before she was left to find her own way. Given simple tasks to preform over the days that grew into weeks, she watched her son grow round. A gurgling coo replaced the pitiful screams. Often Adsheed would be found sitting cross-legged with a child on each breast. Though it was easy to pick her large healthy boy from the stranger who shared, she seemed pleased to have been selected for this duty, growing frustrated only at the lack of a name for the smaller boy.

"Anippe," Ahab-ram said with a sigh to Anippe, who she saw frequently but talked to only when there was something the women could not make clear. "Come with me." He sent the children back and walked with her to a stony hillside where they could sit in peace. "How have you found it here?" He noticed the hollows under her eyes were gone and she seemed to smile more now than the first days.

"It is good. I wish I understood more of what is expected of me, but daily I learn."

"Do you have questions of me before I go on?"

"Only if I will be a wife or concubine?" She looked away, knowing the tent she slept in was of his women. She'd watched nightly as this one or that one left to share his bed, dependent on who Shareefa sent. Embarrassed, she could not meet his eye.

His gentle voice brought her back to him. "I told you, you would be neither slave nor wife or concubine." His outstretched arm encompassed the surrounding area. "This is my tribe, one of many. These are my sheep. These are my children and the children of my wife, Shareefa."

Anippe had already learned that all the children called Shareefa mother, though, perhaps only six were hers by birth.

"My sons come to me from my women or by marrying one of my daughters. My daughters marry here or into other tribes and they go, but the ties stay. I own many sheep and many oases. Soon we will leave here; even now the sheep prepare to move." He paused, looking over his sheep. "There are people of the city who are my people. They came to me to protect your burden, even as I protect my sheep. Here, you will work and live. Though you have been kept secluded thus far, there will be times you will not. Learn well not to speak of other times.

"There are women within my harem that are there by my protection, and few would question them. Indeed, I have even the old, ugly sister of my enemy who would have died when her brother was killed, but I took her. She lives in peace, but her family remembers I spared her life. Samihah, sister to my beloved Shareefa, tells me you are learning quickly. She is promised to my eldest nephew and will leave when our two tribes cross in the desert." Standing, he offered his hand. "The day may come when you leave or your son will go. Until then, you are one of us. Come. Tonight we dance; tomorrow we ride." Pausing with a twinkle in his eye, he said. "Only also this. Your son is now my son in the way of our people. My sweet, round Adsheed is troubled by his lack of name. So, shall he be called Gadi."

Relieved to know she was not to be traded to another,

Anippe smiled, nodding at his choice. She was glad the boy would have a name. Now perhaps they would both have a life.

Great spits roasted whole sheep or goats throughout the camp. Ahab-ram's family consisted of fifty or sixty people and tonight they seemed all gathered in one place. Strange music played. The feasting and dancing went on for many hours. When Anippe woke the next morning, she found the small herd of selected sheep already gone. They would travel while the day was cool. The women were efficiently packing the camp. Everything, including the tents, went on to the camels. Special litters like small rooms held three or four occupants. By mid-morning, they again traveled over the desert.

CHAPTER 26

For two years, Anippe moved from place to place with the tribe. There was a pattern to their traveling that kept them in touch with others like them. The oases that Ahab-ram owned were always open to them while others paid a tithe for the use. He, in turn, negotiated with those who possessed an oasis that he would need to use. Anippe learned to weave, to dye, and to assist with the birthing of both women and sheep. Samihah left with her new husband. Adsheed delivered another son. Shareefa ruled. Gadi grew to toddler. Seated in the shade of a palm, Anippe combed her hair. She thought of her life before; it seemed long ago. More visitors arrived that day; there would be feasting when the men left the tents. Already food cooked and the fermented beverage preferred by the nomads waited.

"Mother, Mother."

She watched Gadi running down the path. His pudgy legs had grown steady and strong. Gathering him into her arms, she tickled him, kissing his face as he giggled. "What do you want, you naughty little boy? Aren't you supposed to be herding lambs?" She loved to touch him. Learning to trust her love for him had not been easy. Now she could barely stand to be separated from him.

"Mother Shareefa says you are to come now." Breathlessly, he fought to escape her hugs and kisses.

Holding hands, they ran back along the path created by thousands of sheep moving through the underbrush for a hundred years. Her laughter faded as they entered the camp area. All around was chaos. Ahab-ram and several of his sons strode out of his private tent. Mounting horses, they whirled, trotting towards the open desert. His face was dark and the heat of his anger could be felt even at this distance.

"Go. Go and find Adsheed. Perhaps she will take you to the lambs," Anippe told her son.

Gadi's hands clung to her for a brief second, but there in the desert he had learned to heed immediately. Unknown fear sent him running, stumbling as he went in search of the comfort Adsheed always offered.

In the tent, Shareefa screamed commands. Tensely, Anippe approached her. Something was very wrong. Tears coursed down the faces of several women. There were no children there. Shareefa and four or five others wore cotton pants in the style of the men.

"Do you have a strong stomach?" she demanded of Anippe.

Nodding, Anippe opened her mouth to ask what was happening.

"Good. Get dressed. We leave in only a few moments."

"Where do we go? Why?" Another helped Anippe pull off her tunic, then offered a much shorter one and pants. She strapped on sandals.

"We go to Ishba, an oasis which is half a day's journey from here."

"Why? What of the others?" Anippe followed Shareefa out of the tent.

Already, women were mounting camels, not in the

ornate litters but in saddles with skins of water and sacks of dried meat strapped on.

"They will follow. There is death."

In the desert, there was always death. This was something different. The camel boys prodded the beasts to their feet and out onto the hot sand. With her robe billowing around her and her face covered against the sun, Anippe rode with the others. The camels did not plod along this time; they were kept trotting even when long strands of saliva frothed from their mouths. The horses were long gone. Here and there, a track still showed. Certainly, this death must be of a high person, for rarely did Ahab-ram allow his beautiful horses to be ridden and never so roughly.

In the mid-afternoon, the oasis came into view. It was small, but lush. The swaying palms were inviting. Rocks littered their route. When they were within five hundred yards of the first green, they could hear the keening of men whose souls were ripped from their chests. The rocks she had seen from the distance upon the sand were actually dead sheep. Sliding off her camel near the central fire pit, bile rose in

Anippe's throat. The cries they had heard were their own men as they moved about the camp area among the dead, men who had been slashed viciously. There were the bodies of women who had been raped and left with their throats cut. Children or pieces of children everywhere.

Throughout the rest of the day, the women and men worked to gather the bodies and prepare them for their journey over the river Styx. As was the way of their people, they wrapped them in gay blankets to be buried out in the desert when darkness fell because there was not enough here to create pyres. Ahab-ram ordered the possessions of his slaughtered people collected. When the mound of tents and furnishings was complete, all were burned. Anippe lay on the hard ground beside the fire pit. This had been only a small family group of perhaps fifteen people, yet the carnage seemed to stretch everywhere. Not only had the people been killed, but so had all the animals except the camels, which were nowhere to be found. Sheep lay everywhere. A few horses had been found slaughtered. Why would someone hurt these gentle desert people and the animals they owned? In the time she had spent among the tribes, she had never witnessed worse than two women fighting over some bauble Ahab-ram had given.

Across the fire, eyes watched hers, seeing the misery grow with the pain that came only from disaster within one's own family; born or taken. It was near dawn before Anippe slept, but still the eyes watched. In the morning, each woman took a blanket and went on to the next gruesome task. They would roll a sheep onto it and then pull it out into the desert, where a mountain of bloated bodies grew. The horses were dragged by camel. Even when the men helped, it was the middle of the afternoon before they were done.

Ahab-ram asked God to forgive his people for not protecting the innocent. He stood before each pile and in his sing-song voice offered his sacrifice. When the piles smoldered, trying to burn, they mounted their beasts, which now carried anything of value left behind by the looters. Through the evening and into the night, they made their way back across the sand. Guards who had encircled the home camp almost casually before now stood tense and ready for danger. Life went on, but it changed.

CHAPTER 27

With the appearance of the next full moon, the time had come

to take the sheep to city markets. They were grown and fat.

This was the closest the tribe traveled to the walled city and

Ahab-ram and his elder sons usually made the journey twice a

year, driving the herds of sheep to the stew pots of the

Egyptians. It was a long and arduous journey that Ahab-ram

made with his sons and perhaps two or three of the women.

While in the city, they would spend days with family that

dwelled there, or wandering the marketplace, gathering gifts

and goods to take back with them. It was laughed around many

campfires that Ahab-ram would even sell his camels given half

a chance, but no one so much as saw the ankle of his woman,

for Shareefa always stayed behind. It was not wise for both of

the portents to be gone at the same time. But in this it seemed changes happened too.

For several weeks, smaller groups of Ahab-ram's family had been arriving at the camp. Men guarded day and night while the bigger boys watched the sheep and goats. Shareefa watched for Samihah and her husband but they did not come.

Shareefa spoke of a Palace of stone Ahab-ram had in the distant mountains. "Many of our people are already on the way there," she said. "They will join together for safety and travel into the hills."

"And what of us?" asked a younger wife.

"When all who have been sent and notice has arrived, the women and children will unite and travel to the mountains."

"We go to the hidden palace?"

Sitting quietly, Anippe listened to the eager voices. They had never seen the horrendous massacres she had at both the Pharaoh's Palace and in the desert. None seemed to understand the danger that encircled them. Only the excitement of this great and glorious journey stirred their blood.

"Yes, you will go. My babies will go also."

"What of you, Shareefa?" asked Anippe. "Won't you travel with us?"

"No, my place is with my husband. Someone will have to stay and take care of the sheep that remain. If all travel together, some who should not know will question why we leave." Her great dark eyes did not show fear, only sadness. "Even now, others band together and move towards the mountains."

The eager girl broke into the talk. "Will we stay long?"

"I don't know. We don't know why our people were attacked." In a low voice, Shareefa gave the others assembled their first real information. "This was not one attack against a small group of nomads. There have been others. And why kill the sheep? They and the oasis are of true value. Yet the oasis was left to spoil by the pillage. Listen to me carefully lest you feel the slash of the knife in the dark. Ahab-ram sends you to safety until he is sure all is well. Keep your eyes and ears open and your mouths shut. Do not allow hysterical babble to be the end of our people."

Shortly after, trays of fruit and sweets were offered before the women prepared for the night. Anippe left the safety of the tent, moving into the soft darkness. Her thoughts roared in her mind. She did not hear the stealthy step of another until a hand touched her shoulder. Jumping away, she pulled a short dagger from her robe.

"Good. That is good. There are many that think you are a foolish Egyptian, but they are wrong." Shareefa's white teeth shone in the night. "Now, come with me."

Startled by Shareefa's touch, Anippe tried to slow her breathing. Between gritted teeth, she exhaled slowly, but it was an effort. Her heart beat like a drum in her ears. She followed Shareefa to the tent of Ahab-ram.

"He has asked for you," said her guide, bowing at the waist as she backed away. The sheer fabric that made up her headpiece and half-veil fluttered on the night breeze. In her cotton tunic, Anippe felt like a peasant compared to the sexual temptress that even now vanished in the shadows. Lifting her chin, she drew aside the tent flap.

"Here now is the woman we spoke of." Ahab-ram sat

surrounded by men strange to Anippe. His beckoning hand drew her to his side. "As I told you, one of my wives is an Egyptian. She came to me sent by a man from a far city. And we have a son, strong and spirited."

Anippe lowered her head demurely, studying her feet. What was this game Ahab-ram played? He did not tell his visitors a lie, but only half truths. Moving back from the circle, she picked up a heated urn. Carefully, she filled each man's goblet. Platters of figs or other fruits lay between the men and, for the rest of the evening, she kept them filled just as she did the goblets. Not another word was spoken to Anippe. Her presence was noted no more than smoke above a burning fire, but the men spoke in the language of her youth. She listened to every word.

"How do you know the Pharaoh searches for this youth?" Ahab-ram asked casually, with a long pull on the communal water pipe. Laughing, he continued. "Perhaps this is just idle gossip from some yearning woman."

"No, I tell you he keeps the High Priest of the old Pharaoh, who was his brother, locked away in a temple near the river." The thin man spoke barely over a whisper. "It is said he does not dare to destroy the Priest because his brother cursed him on this Priest's name."

The shorter man nodded his head emphatically.

"Even the Queen fears the old Priest, and she is the only one Pharaoh trusts to bring him the sacrifices."

Anippe listened to the men's patter with only half her mind. She knew this temple, this palace by the river. So, it had been completed but, instead of a place of pleasure as Manu had prophesied, it was merely a prison. Storage for an old, withered man who lived because he had instilled fear in another.

"This boy exists, I tell you." The short man trembled with his news. "Not all the slaves of the old palace were destroyed. There were some deemed not to be worthy to attend Pharaoh as he traveled in the Chariot across the sky to the gods. These were merely removed from within the palace, either given duties elsewhere in the compound or sold. It takes many to keep Pharaoh's house maintained. It would be foolish to destroy them all." Drinking strongly from his goblet, he leaned forward, speaking in a loud whisper. "For a small amount, I bought two old eunuchs. They had worked in the baths and were very good at wringing the worry from your body at the end of the day. They earned me many coppers in my own bathhouses. But when one lay at the edge of his life, the other, his younger brother, came to me. In exchange for the freedom of his elder brother, he said he had some knowledge that would be beneficial to my purse."

The silence was thick around the men; Anippe's skin prickled.

The man continued his tale. "While he spent his days and nights in the harem caring for the spoiled wives of the old Pharaoh, a new girl was brought. Not a wife, not a concubine as far as he could tell. She was heavy with child. None of the other women bothered with her, but First Wife did. The child was said to be Pharaoh's from a minor Palace. But the eunuch had watched her and First Wife and he believed there was something more. Her hands were worn; she was used to hard work, and made no demands for riches or gifts. On the day of the massacre, these two eunuchs were among the many who had not yet returned to their assigned places. When they did, it was merely to help carry the dead away.

"The old man did not read, but he heard the names of the dead called out. Grieving, he listened to all those who had been the center of his life. Later, he would recall that he had not heard the name of this young girl listed, nor had his brother. Pharaoh searches discretely among the old slaves and the families of the city for something. We believe it is for this woman. It is said a prophecy tells of a woman and a child who escaped the pillage. The child is of royal blood. A soothsayer read my fortune barely hours after the death of this old eunuch and told me a son would rise brighter than that which floats in the heavens. He would come from near but also from afar." Blushing slightly, he added. "I thought my wife, the old whore, would beget a child from another man. When I accused her, she broke a pot over my head."

The dark mood was broken. The men laughed among themselves. Ahab-ram motioned Anippe to leave them and bone dice were produced.

Many small fires burned throughout the oasis community. Anippe sat close to one small fire pit that was more abandoned than the others. Small flames licked upward from the dying embers. The smell of palm smoke, sheep dung, and camel pervaded. In her arms, she held Gadi, sleeping peacefully. His weight was small, no match for the solid stone where her heart had been. In his sleep, he turned like a child, seeking his mother's breast. She cuddled him closer, her hand stroking his exposed hip. A flicker of a smile grew. There was the place that showed he was hers. On his left hip, just below the joint, darker against his dark skin, was a splash of birthmark. Shaped as a droplet of water would be if dropped against a solid surface, the size of her smallest fingernail.

It was this that in a crowd of children would identify him, just as in the crowd of lambs the one with a black ear could be found. He was her lamb. She bent to kiss the small spot, then carried him back to his bed.

Stumbling back to her bed, she thought of what she had heard. It was no coincidence that she was there to pour the wine. By the light of an oil lantern, Shareefa waited for her. Casually, the dark-haired beauty washed herself as all around her slept. The great copper basin threw glints of light about the tent.

"Have you heard what the toothless fool had to say?"

Too numb to speak, Anippe nodded her head miserably. They were not safe here any longer. Gadi had been so happy.

Shareefa watched her intently. She could see Anippe's misery, the indecision worried her. With a firm grasp on Anippe's arm, she drew them both into the center of her great bed. On this night no children slept here, no other woman lay close.

"You must learn to watch your emotions, my daughter, for they are as drawings on the sand across your face." Whispering, she drew Anippe closer so no one could hear. "This is not the first that we have heard of this. Indeed, not long after your arrival, we heard that one who was fearful of torture had spilled the pitiful contents of his head to Pharaoh. A boy who had served the old Pharaoh's Priest and wished for a place with the new spoke of a woman brought into the palace and given to the old Queen. This woman, neither slave nor free, carried a child supposedly Pharaoh's. The old Queen had just seen her only son sent to the land of the dead and her heart accepted this woman's child. Until the birth, woman and unborn babe would live in the harem. After, the woman would go, but the child would remain."

Anippe jerked away from Shareefa. "No. That's not how it was." The whispered words were spoken in anger and indignation.

"You are right. That is probably not how the words were said. But if the Queen were going to keep this child for her own, she would not want another mother present."

Nothing else was said. Shareefa waited for Anippe to work out the thread of what would have actually happened. Tears slowly built in the younger woman's eyes until they spilled down her cheeks. Shareefa continued, "It was even suggested this was the child of the Queen's only son. All knew Pharaoh kept him on a tight leash. He was allowed to practice manhood only where the spilling of his seed would not find fertile ground." She gathered Anippe into her arms. "But he found you. An innocent. And you loved him while he only played at love."

Outside, the wind rose, while Shareefa rocked Anippe,

the foolish slave of Pharaoh, in her arms. This girl who had thought herself so wise, so much slier than the temple occupants. Tears that had remained locked within her for the years of her life spilled over until she succumbed to exhaustion and slept among the embroidered pillows in the arms of the desert queen.

CHAPTER 28

The last days before Ahab-ram would leave for the city had arrived. With her new knowledge, Anippe saw the changes taking place in families around her as they prepared to be seperated. Then there was the sorting of sheep. Which ones would stay and which would go, a chore she had previously believed to be done randomly. The best kept separating to leave with the groups headed further away toward safety. Additional members of Ahab-ram's people had arrived, swelling the numbers, before breaking apart and moving on.

She witnessed the private and tearful moments as women who must leave were torn from men who would stay with the small herd of remaining sheep. A whispered conversation behind a tent wall by two who did not know she eavesdropped explained that to desert the many oases held by

Ahab-ram would mean the permanent loss of great wealth. Anippe had been here for a long while, but her eyes were newly opened. Messengers came and went; no one pointed her out or slyly watched her movements. She could feel the tension of a race of people embarking on an unknown quest and she felt guilt.

When Ahab-ram announced on the last day that only men would be going to the Pharaoh's city this time, he was met with the foul temper of those still in his household. Shareefa stood aside, saying not a word until they were closeted together. His ears would ring for a very long time following that interview. After the chief woman stamped from her lord's tent, another who had been sitting quietly unnoticed entered.

Anippe walked gracefully until standing directly before the still red-faced man. She dropped to the floor, face pressed into the thick carpet in supplication.

"What is it, child?" He growled.

Sitting back on her heels, she met his gaze without trepidation. "It is time for me to return." She stated matter-of-factually. She had expected an argument, but none came.

"Will you stay in the city when I return?" he asked.

"Yes, but free of your protection. I do not wish to turn your generosity into a death sentence."

"The child will remain here."

Anippe nodded, unable to trust her voice. It was good he did not ask her if she had a plan, for she had none. Fate called her back to the horrors she had left behind.

So it was, when the camels and sheep moved out on to the desert sand at midnight on the following evening, one garbed as a young boy rode with them. Surrounded by the family that had accepted her without question, she grieved dry-eyed at the separation, perhaps forever, from her son.

Within the city walls, she became a minor female relative ensconced, in the home of a distant uncle. Ahab-ram sold his sheep then rode back into the desert, leaving her behind with only a small pouch of coins.

CHAPTER 29

One of the women in the uncle's household was Yasii. She was
of a good heart but had been cursed at birth with a harelip. To
prevent offending others, she went about constantly veiled. Her
fingers were quick and diligent. Few could create embroidery
as fine as hers, and for this, she was employed by the women
of many households. When she would finish work in one place,
she was quickly absorbed somewhere else. It was her fate,
however, not to be accepted as a permanent resident by one of
her benefactors because of her affliction. There was much
superstition surrounding the stigma of a harelip, and though
she was a beautiful and talented girl, she would never know a
husband, children, or home of her own.

Being of a similar age, Anippe and Yasii became great
friends. Anippe spoke of her desert home but never shared her

knowledge of the city or that she had a son. Because she needed to find a spot or allow the uncle to marry her off, Anippe questioned the other woman about how she succeeded in her own enterprise.

Eyes sparkled above the ornate veil. "If you want to be your own mistress, you must have something to offer. What have you?" Yasii asked.

Anippe offered her own embroidery with its intricate original patterns.

Yasii's eyes grew large. "Oh, you of hidden talents," she cried. "We go tomorrow to the commerce quarter."

Accompanied by Yasii, Anippe proceeded to the Avenue of Tailors to wait in the pre-dawn rustle of commerce. Women of known quantity whose quality of work was good were selected quickly, while others were snubbed by the Domos looking for day workers. Sitting on a small mat, Anippe spread out the bits and pieces of her work before her, samples of her knowledge. Yasii sat near her, sharp eyes peering in the growing light for the representative of Pharaoh, for it was within Pharaoh's walls that true wealth and a fair price could be had.

Finally, the red fez with gold trim and bright red caftan of Yahamen was spotted sweeping along the stones. Frowning slightly, Anippe watched his advance. She expected him to be accompanied by many retainers, but other than two clerks, he appeared to be alone. Alone, that was, until the impudent ran to him, throwing themselves at his feet and clutching at his robes. Then, as though summoned by Ra, great, burly Nubian guards materialized from the crowd. Naked save for the silken trousers whose billowing folds started below their navel and ended in tight ankle cuffs, their only other garb was great curved scimitars. Oiled muscles barely rippling, they tossed the unfortunate aside.

"Ha." Hissed Yasii. "They will have no hope this day. Quickly, quickly, put out your fine seams. Cast not your eyes on Yahamen."

A flurry about her told Anippe that others also employed this trick. For a moment, hope fled her chest.

Known already to him, Yahamen did not hesitate before Yasii, merely grunting for her to follow. Grabbing up her mat quickly, she rushed to his far side, forcing others closer to him and they, in turn, pushed the Domo to Anippe. With her eyes downcast to a point just in front of her ankles, she saw only his sandaled feet and polished toenails hesitate.

A be-ringed hand snatched up her fine seam. A soft clucking sound confused her before an impudent clerk asked, "Is this your work?"

"Yes, master."

Another cluck. "You come."

She picked up her mat, joining those selected. Neither Anippe nor Yasii spoke.

Once inside the Palace walls, the women were left to the head tailor, a fat, greasy Persian whose teeth were yellow and cracked. He had no fear of a woman's scrutiny, for his extremely foul breath kept them far away. All he approached turned their heads away, burying noses in their scarves.

Anippe worked efficiently on her assigned piece, thankful for the knowledge she had gained in this same palace as a child. Other women sat about her, including Yasii, chatting and giggling as they worked. Day workers were segregated from those who lived in the palace. The women gathered daily to assist in the miles of stitching, but never got past the servant quarters. The roofed pavilion under its intricately carved colonnades and with its bubbling fountain would be all they would see. Those who came with them would be all they would meet except for the tailor and the kitchen slaves, who at mid-morning arrived carrying a huge copper kettle.

Food left from the repast of Palace residents was dumped into huge vats, stewed until all identity was lost, then fed to the minions. Each woman set before her a wooden beggar's bowl, an item they carried hidden in the folds of their robes. Into each, the kitchen slaves dumped a quantity of stew. Pharaoh could afford to be generous with this sludge left from his tables. For many, this would be the only meal they would have that day. They were entitled to it merely by being chosen to work in the palace. If they were to earn additional wages, it was dependent on the volume and quality they turned out in the eleven or twelve hours they worked. Yasii, like many others, picked at the food, wrapping a cloth around it to keep the flies off. What they did not eat, they would take home to their children.

Anxious to keep Yasii free from any association with her should her plan fail, Anippe sat a distance away, speaking only to those who sat immediately beside her. Occasionally, their eyes met. A furtive meeting of two with the same thought.

As dusk fell, the Domo, with the tailor at his elbow, walked among the women, inspecting the work. In the same soft voice, the strange clucking became the dialect of his home, instructing the clerk how much to pay.

Weeks passed as the two women would leave the home of Yasii, making their separate way to the same place, then home again. Strangers outside of their own walls.

Yahamen decided who was hired daily, but the tailor decided who would be assigned the more lucrative tasks. Not wanting to encourage the malodorous Persian, Anippe allowed him to believe she returned every evening to the home of her husband, a large and vile tempered man. She did, however, allow him to lean over her as she worked to create tiny, even stitches. So fine was her work that he allowed her to work on the veils of Pharaoh's lesser wives and concubines because the resident seamstress worked only for the Queen of Pharaoh. Every day as she worked, Anippe left a small mat she carried with her spread on the ground in clear view.

As Yahamen circled the room, Anippe continued to stitch, surveying the small amount of work she had to show for the day. Those who knew his ways, and wished to be called forth again, showed their gratitude by working earnestly until he stopped before them. She saw his feet approach, then move smoothly past. Frowning, she continued to stitch even as she heard others pick up their mats and leave.

Moving around the room, the tailor's assistants collected the work left behind, separating the finished work from the other. Anippe gave up her work regretfully. The pavilion was almost empty. She sat alone in the late sun, bowing her head at the approach of many feet.

"Woman."

She raised her eyes, pulling the edge of her shawl across her face. Yahamen had addressed her directly. "Yes, master."

"This is your work? Your design?"

"Yes, master."

Behind him, the tailor stood, sweat running down the side of his face. Beneath the long sleeves of his robe, he nervously rubbed his hands together. Five other people stood behind him, two eunuchs, a fat woman, and two other adult women.

"Explain the message to me."

Handing her the mat she had carefully worked, he stepped back, causing the others to move in a semi-circle before her. The fat woman center-most.

Anippe lay the cloth out on the floor. Kneeling behind it, she spoke in a clear voice. "This is Pharaoh." She pointed to the seated man wearing the mask of Ra, then pointed to the man and woman kneeling on the other side of the circle. "These are the people of Egypt whose lives are graced by the bounty of Pharaoh." Pausing momentarily, she cupped her hands around the center figure, a woman slim but not tall who stood on a block of cut stone. At her feet was a water skin. She offered sheaves of wheat and a butchered fowl. Rays of yellow emanated from her form towards the kneeling pair.

"Between Pharaoh and all the lands he rules, is the wife of Pharaoh." The fat woman with her food-stained skirt moved closer, bending over to peer at the diagram.

Lowering her voice slightly, Anippe spoke directly at the top of the other woman's head. "The wife of Pharaoh is the mother of all his children; she is the mother of all the people of Egypt. Here is our mother, representative of Pharaoh, loved by the people. The water of the Nile is at her feet for her to share. The food and animals of the Earth she gathers to feed the hungry. See these rays of light? It is her goodness and her generosity spreading out to all the people."

Silence settled as the woman continued to scrutinize the fabric glyph. Grunting, she stood and spoke. "It does not look like me."

Lowering her eyes, Anippe spoke to Yahamen. It was not befitting that she addressed the Queen of Egypt. "I am sorry, mistress. Time did not allow the fine work needed to present a true picture. Only the stark outline of one whose beautiful heart carves a picture of her grace deep within our souls."

The Queen waggled her fingers at the cloth then turned to leave. The eunuchs and one woman left with her.

In his soft voice, the Domo addressed Anippe. "Queen Kanika is pleased with your work."

Anippe's bowed head nodded slightly. "She would have you stitch a banner flag for her." Anippe nodded, going rigid as Yahamen continued. "During the time it will take for you to finish this piece, you will reside in the palace dormitories. In this manner, the Queen will be able to inspect your work at her leisure. You may send Phanin to notify your family."

"I have no family," whispered Anippe.

"Your husband?" interrupted the tailor.

"The father of my child is dead. My child is no longer, and I do not know of my family."

The tailor who had perceived this husband was furious. "Where have you lived then?"

A twinkle appeared in Yahamen's eye at the tailor's tirade. It was not his way to worry about those whose lives were beneath his, but the red face and shaking body of the obese and dirty Persian amused him. Few people who had business with the tailor did not know of his lecherous manner.

"Behind the market, master, behind the fruit stands."

"You .. you told me..." The tailor's sputtering stopped when he realized she had never actually said anything.

Many duties awaited the Domo. Leaving a clerk behind, he moved on.

The tailor also left, but the slap of his sandals on the stone bespoke his irritation.

Throwing a few coins on the mat, the clerk stated. "For today. You will be compensated for the Queen's banner when it is done, dependent on the time you live on the bounty of Pharaoh and the quality of your work. Go with Phanin. She will show you your place."

Just like the Domo and the tailor, the clerk did not ask if Anippe wished for this task. It was the wish of the Queen, therefore, so it would be. Anippe had prayed for an entry into the palace with its inner world, but she had not expected to live within its walls. She gave thanks as she followed the other woman along the beautiful mosaic tile walk.

CHAPTER 30

The next weeks were hectic. Anippe was re-introduced to the Queen's seamstresses' quarters. As she expected, there was no one there she knew. When Phanin left her with the only introduction being by order of Queen Kanika, the other women turned their backs on her. She was an interloper, perhaps a spy, not to be trusted or included in their lives. She ate the burned crusted remains from the blackened pot and slept where she found room without so much as a tattered blanket about her. During the time she waited for the Queen to accept the rough design done with charcoal on papyrus, she hemmed or stitched, anything she found waiting to be done.

At last the Queen's head woman returned with a message stating Anippe's design pleased the wife of Pharaoh, so work began. Anippe carefully selected her threads and fabrics, working diligently in almost total silence. Still shunned by the other women, which was no concern to her, she sat near the edge of the hall doorway listening to the sounds without.

Because of her ponderous bulk, Queen Kanika traveled in her sedan chair even through the long corridors of her Palace. Anippe's keen ear soon became attuned to the sounds of the bearers' feet as they slapped down the staircase. In turn, Anippe used this for her own ends. Though she had no clear plan, the nagging idea that she needed to be here persisted.

When the Queen's chair passed, the young woman would wait several minutes, then, grabbing up her basket of work, she would hurry after her benefactor. Her seemingly hurried steps, however, never allowed her to catch up to the Queen's procession. When questioned, she honestly spoke her name, stating that she was on the Queen's business with the need to catch up with the rest of the party. A ruse that did not fail her.

Hours were spent within the walls of the new palace memorizing the layout. Much had changed; there was construction everywhere. Where once huge open areas had been the norm, now there were gates or doors, small rooms that seemed to have no purpose. New statuary and ponderous potted plants changed the landscape. It was confusing, but before she could trust herself to look deeper into the reason she was here, Anippe was certain she needed to know how best to get out.

On one of her earlier forays, she saw the old hall sweeper. He did not acknowledge her, nor she, him.

Queen Kanika allowed her head-woman to schedule small tasks to relieve the royal women's boredom. One of these appointments was the schedule of jewelers, wig-makers, and the stitchers who worked on items the Queen had ordered. Sure that this was just a way for the head-woman to occupy her petty mistress, Anippe would arrive with her work as instructed. One day, the Queen presented her with a lovely teal silk vest that Anippe believed to have been made for a lessor wife. The embroidery was fine, and the piece was a very good fit. Anippe thanked her benefactor profusely, then proceeded to put the vest in her basket.

"Put it on." Hissed the head-woman.

Hesitantly, Anippe pulled the vest out, stroking the luxurious fabric again as though loath to put it aside.. It was hard to tell what the tiny eyes ensconced in rolls of fat were actually looking at, but Anippe would see. If she had offended the Queen in a small way, then perhaps a larger display would rectify the issue. Anippe made a great show of putting the vest on over her plain unbleached tunic, taking several minutes to tug it straight, while repeatedly running her hands over the silk. With a sigh of pleasure, Anippe caressed the garment one last time before picking up her basket to leave.

A sly smile appeared on the face of the reclining woman. Though Anippe would have sworn she was sleeping, like a fat crocodile, the older woman lay among her pillows, watching. After that, Anippe wore the vest whenever she left the fabric vault.

CHAPTER 31

Comfortable now with her ability to find her way around the several Palace buildings, Anippe ventured further. One of the major changes was the removal of the guest harem from the Queen's Palace. Visitors were now housed in what had previously been the children's building. The children now lived on the second floor, directly beneath the harem. Here, they had more access to their mothers. It was a more favorable arrangement. Also, the harem occupants had open access to the river terrace and the roof area unless the Queen specifically restricted the area.

The women here now were rowdy and loud. Fights were not uncommon, with some losers suffering mighty wounds. Though still maintained to the high standards by armies of slaves, Anippe noticed a slightly shabby feeling that she could not quite identify. It seemed as though the tall piles of stone were saddened by their new fate.

This Queen also would not remain in her quarters, waiting to be summoned. Daily she went to the Judicial Hall listening while Pharaoh sorted out the problems of state. It was another place Anippe followed her to. This proved to be a mistake. The lithe girl in her bright teal vest was seen often hurrying along in the wake of the golden sedan. Eventually some noticed. Though most just smiled at the fleet-footed servant, one did not. Constantly, watching for a fresh game, Manu, Pharaoh of Egypt, Lord of the Night Sky, perceived this young woman as an object of his ownership.

"Who is that tardy girl that follows you?" he questioned his wife as she shoved a whole dove's breast into her mouth. Her greasy fingers reached for a wine goblet. When it toppled, she slammed her fist against the low table for another.

"Huh?" She did not care why her husband would want to know. She was secure with two sons and an infant daughter wailing in the nursery.

"The girl in the blue vest." He tried to be casual, but the

sight of his gluttonous wife made his juices run.

Her sly eyes peered up at him. "Are you being naughty, Lord?" she asked.

"Would you care?" he parried.

"Only if you did not allow me to watch." Her coarse laugh spewed food morsels before her. She had her own entertainment; she could afford to be generous. "It's a good thing you asked when you did, my pet." Slaves worked to wipe the grease from her short, pudgy fingers. "She was brought here to create a banner for me. She is a fine seamstress. Her work is done and she will be leaving soon. Perhaps even on the morrow." Hefting her bulk, she moved toward her sedan. "Perhaps you had better take your repast tonight alone." Gurgling happily, she settled her girth for the ride back to her divan and a well-deserved afternoon nap.

Stories of Pharaoh's lecherous appetite had reached Anippe's ears shortly after her arrival. Though eventually she would have to deal with him, she was not prepared to do so now. This had been only a scouting mission from which she expected to return to the desert and her son while Ahab-ram devised a plan for them.

Late afternoon found Anippe striding through the stone archways. The setting sun cast shadows of blue into black or violet, about her creating a world of writhing shadows. It had been her habit for many weeks to share her meal at the slaves' kitchens. The food and the company appealed to her better, and gossip was an aid. Returning from her meal, she moved in the purposeful way of her youth, not comfortable to just casually stroll along.

One shadow detached itself from another. On bare feet, it moved after its quarry. The attacker, used to the submissive behavior of Palace slave girls, was not prepared for the twisting yank that pulled his arm hard in the socket. He had reached with one large paw to grasp Anippe's upper arm. At his first touch, she had thrown herself around, pulling him off balance. She brought the heel of her free hand up hard against his chin, the force of her stiff arm behind it.

A light flashed in his eyes as his teeth slammed together. Coughing, he grabbed again. This time, he caught the side of her head, slamming her onto the floor. The momentum slid her into a fountain. A trickle of blood ran from her temple. It did not enfeeble her; only fear could slow her now, but it could also empower her. He again pounced. She rolled on to her back, bringing her feet up. As he landed on her, she bent her knees and grasped his belt. Before his movement stopped, she pushed her strong legs up, sending her attacker over her head. Springing to her feet, she darted to the side. Her attacker clawed at her tunic, grasping fabric but not flesh. The sound of ripping cloth was unnoticed.

There was no room to maneuver here, for the inner wall was too close. Anippe darted behind one of the six-foot braziers, which burned day and night to add light. Pharaoh's henchman held tight to the cloth. Anippe cornered tight around the burning brazier. She felt the tunic catch on the intricate brass ornament. Still on his knees, the man held tight. She moved towards him, yanking mightily on the remnants of her garment. Then, as the brass started to topple, she darted aside, sliding on the polished stone.

Hot oil poured onto the man's outstretched arms, barely missing his face. His high-pitched screams followed as he ran down the corridor.

The girl ran in the opposite direction. At the entry to the fabric vault, she collapsed. The sound of her body falling to the floor and her gasping breath drew the inhabitants. For the first time, the old women looked at her with interest. Taking her arms, two dragged her inside. The third silently closed the doors after making sure her pursuer was not in sight. Cleaning her injuries before offering her wine, they sat with her until she slept.

When she awoke in the morning, one woman sat beside her. As Anippe's eyes flickered open, her attendant whispered, "It is not safe for you here, girl. Already, men prowl the corridors, seeking you. We have turned them away, but it will not last."

Groaning with pain, Anippe tried to sit, but the elder pushed her back. "Stay here, rest. When the mid-day comes, take your things and go. Do not be seen, for we all shall die." After speaking about her concerns, the old woman crept away.

Anippe found herself hidden in a tunnel created by bolts of fabrics. There was water and her repaired tunic. Her meager belongings were bundled near her.

CHAPTER 32

When the sun hit its zenith and all who could, found a place
out of the burning heat to rest, Anippe crept out of her hiding
spot. She was not foolish enough to believe Manu would allow
her to stroll through the palace and out the main gate. Her
biggest challenge was to first leave this place for one where
she would have more anonymity. Her tunic was in ruins.
Pulling her vest on to cover the repairs done to the damage of
the previous evening, she searched for her best means of
escape. The main corridor was busiest as tradesman moved
about as well as palace occupants.

Gathering together a large basket filled with material,
she piled it high enough to cover her lower face. With the
attitude of one who had every right to venture forth, she
stepped into the traffic, moving along the main corridor.

Walking its length, she forced herself to breathe. She remembered that once before; she had hoped to escape the palace. With eyes downcast, she moved down the broad steps. Here the way was even busier. Relieved, she moved a little quicker.

A high-pitched voice behind cut her off. "Stop, girl."

Turning, she found a youth, probably newly initiated into Pharaoh's guard. "It is the command of Manu, Pharaoh of all that inhabit the land, that you attend him."

She could see no quick escape. "As Pharaoh wishes," she murmured. "Only, please, I was told by Queen Kanika to bring these to the Chief of the harem."

The boy-man stood uncertain if he should take a chance crossing the outspoken Queen, known for her vicious temper, or follow Manu's command. The doorway was only a few feet away. Anippe waited. "Go," he said. "Be quick."

Anippe hurried through the lattice-carved archway. The Pharaoh's messenger remained in the wide corridor believing Anippe would deposit her armful of fabrics, then return.

Barely able to breathe past the fist-sized knot of fear

filling her throat, Anippe dropped the basket of cloth as soon as she was out of sight and ran to the door, which opened to the side alley.

Peering around the corner from the small hall into the main corridor, she spied the young soldier pacing nervously in front of the door she had entered. When his head was turned away, she darted out, hoping to hide among others traveling the Palace walkways. She was unaware that her vivid teal silk vest was a flag heralding her departure. Even as she darted to the left, a shout raised behind her followed by the slap of leather on marble as the guard followed in pursuit. The corridor of fountains was crowded with the guests of Pharaoh and their retinues. Today, a cool spot was difficult to find and the musical tinkling of water and occasional spray offered oasis.

Slowing her steps, Anippe melded in with a family trailing an obese Punjab. His many wives giggled at her presence. Frantic to be hidden, she shushed them and pointed behind at the frantically searching young man. Still the women giggled, but as one they closed in around her, fluttering their veils and gauzy shawls, hiding Anippe in a colorful swirl.

When their slow parade passed a small archway Anippe knew led outside, she slipped from the group. Moving at a pace that would not attract attention, she followed a path she hoped would take her away from those who perhaps still sought her. Her tension subsided slightly, allowing clear thoughts to form. She had wanted Pharaoh to notice her, but on her terms. This unexpected summons could not be good.

Bright light burst onto her face. Unintentionally, she'd arrived in a courtyard where slaves gathered for their daily meal.

Where should I go? She wondered, looking over the lines of white garbed servants.

Those who had filled their bowls milled around, settling in friendly groups on the stone benches or ground. A commotion erupted nearby as her pursuers shoved others out of their way. One eunuch, a giant among his peers, took offense, innocently allowing Anippe time to escape. Irrational haze cloaked her vision. She stumbled through the lines of slaves until a rough hand yanked her to the ground. As she fought to escape, her captor ripped off the bright vest, leaving her in the same white shift as everyone else in the courtyard.

"Let me go." she gasped.

"Quiet. Sit still." The man ordered, shoving her vest into his tunic. He pushed a worn wooden bowl half filled with gruel into her hand. "Eat. Do not look up."

Those about them did not notice, for many heads were turned to the pummeling given by the eunuch to the Pharaoh's messenger.

Lifting the bowl to her mouth, Anippe turned her head toward the noise. Immediately, the man pushed her head down.

"Do not cast your gaze towards your enemy," he growled. "Do you know nothing? As your eyes seek, so shall his. They will reveal your soul, calling him to you."

"Who are you?" she whispered. On the edge of her vision, she saw the messenger stumble away, his face a bloody mask.

"I am no one you know but one who has known of you before."

For a few minutes, they were safe. When her bowl was empty, he put it into a woven basket. From the same basket, he pulled a soft mohair shawl, faintly green in color. Placing it around her shoulders, he took her arm, drawing her after him.

"I am not going with you!" Anippe protested.

"If I leave you here, you will be dead by morning. And my father will be very angry," he said, speaking softly. "The man that pursued you will return to his master and say you were here but not to be found. Then he and those who are of his Eridinii will hunt for you."

"Pharaoh is his master."

"Then we had better hurry."

"Why would you save me?" she asked with a gasp.

"I have been watching for you." His grin had a wicked hint. "I was told to watch for a desert storm within these walls."

Wrapped in the soft folds of wool with downcast eyes, Anippe followed the man from one hard-packed sand avenue to another. Their way led to the area where merchants were allowed to display their wares. Most were gone, but a boy and girl who looked to be of thirteen or fourteen years squatted beside four camels. The camels were lightly loaded, which bespoke of a prosperous day.

Taking the lead rope, the man hoisted Anippe onto the camel, then mounted another. The two youths did not question her appearance, merely clamoring on to the other beasts. Anippe's rescuer grunted a command, putting all into motion. "Hut, hut."

Among the jingling of tiny bells and the soft clop of plodding feet, they rode through the Palace gates into the city.

The city sprawled for many miles under the hot Egyptian sun. Traffic was thick in the area near the Palace but grew less as they moved toward down lesser traveled streets. The soft crush of darkness was on them before the camels' jogging pace slowed. They were well past the outskirts of the city and into the desert when Anippe first noticed the difference in the beasts' behavior. No longer patiently following, now the three behind vied to be first. Only the large male remained calm, but even he chirped happily. They were home.

Expecting the hut of the peddler, here far from the city, to be meager and poor, Anippe's wondering gaze beheld a vast compound with paddocks and tents surrounding. Before them, tall wooden gates slowly opened. Oil lamps burned throughout the courtyard, swinging in the night breeze and lighting the way of those who hurried about to finish the last of the day's work. Several boys ran forward to unload the packs and baskets hanging from the camel's harnesses. Like rickety old women, the great beasts sank to the ground, their chittering calls answered by others corralled near the gates.

Standing uncertainly beside her mount, Anippe listened to the cheerful greeting given to her hosts while men and women alike bantered about them. A toddler of perhaps three ran to the girl, squeaking in delight. He was quickly scooped up and covered with kisses as his old nursemaid stood patiently, waiting. Still hugging her child tightly, the young mother motioned Anippe to leave her beast to the herd boy and follow her. Talk swirled about her. Though the dialect sounded familiar, she did not understand the words. This was not a humble dwelling where all would eat from a community pot, but a Palace grand enough for a minor nobleman.

Once inside the inner courtyard with its walls of man-made stone, the child was handed back to his nurse, who carried him away.

"Come this way."

Anippe started in surprise. This was the first time she had been spoken to since leaving the Palace. "Where are we?" she asked.

"This is the home of my father, Abu Ben Hageed. He will no doubt see you later."

Her guide moved into a smaller room, letting the curtain fall over the doorway. Three young girls ran forward, bowing at the waist, offering a sing-song greeting.

"I am Rahaf," said the young woman. "We will bathe, then eat." Her robe was already a puddle around her feet. She stepped into a large, low bowl made from a tanned hide. She continued to chat with Anippe as the girls, naked except for a loincloth, oiled and scraped her body.

After the cleaning process was complete, the two women were rubbed down vigorously with rough towels, then cooled by ostrich feathered fans. Finally, there was a lapse in Rahaf's ongoing monologue describing the customs of her people and what Anippe could expect through the evening.

Groping for conversation while she tried to remember everything she had been told, Anippe asked about the child. "Was that your son? He is quite handsome, but you are very young." Immediately, she realized she had been rude. Rahaf merely giggled.

"I am not young; only do I look so. That is why I was selected to go with Hakeem to the harem." She touched Anippe's arm. "It is no place for a youth who would bring danger by indiscretion. He is my son. I have another also, but he is still a babe."

"And was the man your father?" Anippe asked shyly.

This time, all the women laughed.

"I will not tell him you asked that. He will be mortally offended." Rahaf smiled broadly. "Hakeem is my brother. The other is my brother as well. He is young, but a quick learner." A gong sounded in the distance. "Come, we go to eat."

Dressed in the amok Rahaf had given her, Anippe stood among the women, waiting for the small side door to open and allow them entrance to the center hall. This temple to the tribe, with its high vaulted ceiling, was the most important place in the compound. On their entrance, the women silently encircled the outside wall to sit on flat mats facing an inner wall which was eighteen inches high. Until the time the head wife decided to leave, they would sit quietly while the men visited and dined. All the women would gather for a meal after the men had finished. Many, Anippe and Rahaf included, had taken a light repast with the children for their evening meal. This ruse did not follow decorum, but was universally overlooked.

Hidden behind the heavy veil she was required to wear, Anippe surveyed the room. Stout columns rose to the ceiling. Each depicted, she was to learn, the life story of some auspicious ancestor. Carvings swirled from bottom to top, depicting birth to death those who were honored. The gentle swaying of brightly colored banners hanging from the ceiling told of the rise of desert winds wafting through the open roof. The banners kept the sun off those inside while light shone through or stars twinkled, waiting for an admiring glance.

Low divans and large cushions were scattered about, each serviced by a low table on which slaves placed platters and full goblets. Many of the divans were already claimed by a male family member. The youngest appeared to be the boy who had been with them from the Palace. In the center of the room on cushions stacked on a raised platform reclined a wizened man, dark as teak and wrinkled as a date. His swarthy appearance spoke of years exposed to hot sun and biting winds. Only men of thirteen years and older sat or reclined in the center area. There were no children in the room. The women of the family sat on colorful mats around the outer walls, fully covered by their amok. Though slaves moved about the room, placing platters of food on the low tables within easy reach of the men, the women would not eat while in attendance.

Lithe girls swirled to the flutes and finger cymbals moving in unison while avoiding collision with those bearing trays of spicy-scented treats. Strong male laughter erupted at the entry as Hakeem strolled through the carved archway with four others. He no longer wore his coarsely woven striped robe, white cotton trousers, and camel hair fez. Now maroon trousers of silk gathered below his navel, flowing to his ankles where the embroidered cuff fit snugly. He wore no shirt, but his short vest was decorated with heavy embroidery, the glitter of jewels accenting the wide expansion of flesh. His skin was dark and curly black hair crossed his chest, then followed a tapering stream down past his navel, over his taut belly, and disappearing in the low waistband of his pants. The five men strode directly to the elder. Only Hakeem did not drop to the ground. Instead, he bowed at the waist. Touching his fingers reverently to his forehead, he paused before seating himself at his father's right. The old man, master of it all, graciously spoke with any who left their comfort to approach him.

Hakeem was only slightly taller than the others in his group, but he seemed to shine past them. His black hair curled from behind his ears. Sharp facial features were balanced by a square, clean-shaven chin. Gold bands encircled his bulging upper arms. Anippe's mouth dried as her gaze danced over this man who had rescued her.

He looked about the room, but she could not tell if his gaze noted the women. Anippe watched in amazement as he took food from the old man's platter. She was certain no one else would dare. Not once did he look in her direction. His talk was jovial, including everyone in range. For a long while she sat stiffly until the Head-Wife rose discreetly to leave the men to their water pipes and comforts.

Anippe felt her bowels quiver with exhaustion. She declined food, so Rahaf took her to a sleeping room, a small, windowless cell whose only comfort was a narrow platform stacked with sheep skins against the cold desert night. She would be safe there, Rahaf told her, for the one corridor entrance was guarded by two great mustached Arabians and an equally broad woman. Shivering uncontrollably, Anippe burrowed into the fleece.

"What have I done? Where is my son?" Words repeated and repeated again carried her to a dreamless sleep.

Sometime during her sleep, Rahaf came to gaze at Anippe sadly while the oil lamp was refilled so it would burn brightly while she slept.

It was late morning when the Egyptian struggled awake. She felt dazed, confused. The air was heavy and close. Stepping into the corridor, the sound of water splashing and female chatter drew attention to a common washing area.

There were sandstone basins filled and emptied by silent slaves.

Rahaf sat with others on low benches while her hair was brushed, then wound into innumerable slim, tight braids. She patted the seat next to her. "I thought you would sleep until the afternoon."

On the previous evening no one had questioned Anippe, now others hovered close. Rahaf provided a clean robe scented with sandalwood and cloves. When she was refreshed, her hostess led her to a wide archway where Hakeem loitered against the stone.

A welcoming smile lit his face. "Good Morning. I am hopeful you rested well?" At her nod, he drew her further into the room. "My father awaits within. This is a good place for us to talk. No one can approach that we cannot see."

A few slaves stood near the dais. Other than that only the old man was present. He smiled, showing his few remaining teeth, the color of old ivory. Hakeem bowed before him, directing Anippe to a cushion at the Chieftain's feet.

"Welcome, child." He sounded hoarse, his voice a

rough croak. "Do you wonder how you are here?"

Anippe found her voice. The setting was intimate. She took the chance the men would not find offense. "I am grateful for your assistance, for surely I would be suffering even as we speak. But why? Why did you help me? Why do you seem to know me when I do not know you?"

The elder waved to his son with the casual air of one used to instant response. Hakeem waited until an approaching slave placed a small platter beside Anippe, then withdrew. Besides the goblet of precious water, there were figs, pitted dates stuffed with nut meats, and olives shining from soaking in their own juice.

When Anippe looked up, the three of them were alone. Selecting a stuffed fig, she took a small bite. In silence, the two young people watched the elder. He sat with his head back against a misty green cushion, contemplating the sun beyond the fluttering silk banners, each one artfully hand-painted with a prayer to a different god. When he at last moved to look at his guest, she noticed the slight rheumy cast in his wise eyes. The previous evening, the old master's advanced years had not gone unnoticed, but now he appeared to be older than she had previously thought.

"We are instructed that all men are to be as brothers. If our brothers are hungry, we offer substance; if our brothers are besotted with plague, we offer cleansing." His eyes held hers. "If our brothers live in ignorance, we offer the teachings of Allah. In this manner, our family is large. We know of the workings in each household, no matter the distance, no matter the issue." Silence filled the room.

Anippe considered the words of Abu Ben Hageed. Lost in her thoughts, she started when fingers lightly touched her elbow. Laying among his pillows again, her host's eyes were closed. She was unsure if he was meditating or sleeping.

Hakeem and Anippe stepped back into the sunlight, where Rahaf waited patiently. Smiling innocently, she glided up to the pair. Her knowing eyes saw the faint blush flowing from Anippe's chest to her cheeks when she caught Hakeem's gaze. There was also a glint of interest found in her brother's face.

"I thought to walk with you," Rahaf said, smiling

demurely. "You may be here for many days and need to know our home."

While Rahaf spoke, Anippe listened intently, but when she acknowledged what had been said, she did so in Egyptian.

"Do you find our speech difficult?" Hakeem asked.

"It is not easy for me to grasp the trick of tongues," Anippe confessed.

"Hm." Rahaf frowned. "We learn early because, as you see, we are a mixed household."

"As is the palace," Anippe continued, dropping her hands helplessly. "I was there a long time. I just did not seem to learn."

"What do you know?" asked Rahaf gently.

"Besides the Pharaoh's Egyptian, I speak the dialect of the people, also Hebrew, and some Arabic, though I understand more than I can speak in two or three dialects." In the melting pot of the capital city, this was not much. "And I read glyphs."

"You read!" Hakeem and Rahaf gasped in surprise.

"Glyphs." Anippe stammered, watching the others nervously. "I-I asked. Some knew one, maybe two. I paid attention and remembered."

Hakeem's laugh bellowed, startling small birds from the archway. With a short bow, he departed. Anippe blushed again, this time with embarrassment.

"Ah," Rahaf said with a smile. "He is impressed, my brother. You are perhaps the only female he knows who can read." Putting her head close, she whispered. "It is a sly thing to read the language of Pharaoh." Giggling, she drew the other woman along.

Once again, the curiosity of children came to Anippe's aid. The compound encompassed several acres around an area where stone mountains hidden under the sand had burst forth. This area included three wells that had been guarded zealously for generations. The common well, the only one most visitors ever knew of, was situated in the courtyard. The stone wall was only three feet high, but the well, six feet across, was broad and deep. From the children who followed her continually, she learned it had never gone dry. Every time water was drawn, a small amount was poured back in gratitude. It was a superstitious behavior honored by all.

Tradesman and visitors arrived daily. It was easily obtained knowledge that Abu Ben Hageed's grandfather had once been a lowly middleman between the caravan drivers and the merchants. Now, his sons owned those same caravans. They also owned the shopkeepers and the ear of the man who served the palace, a Major Domo Loust.

When the burning sun was at its highest, the residents of the desert Palace took time from their duties to rest, some in the small enclosed cubicles in which they slept but most grouped together near the fountains. Many of the large open porticoes with their great columns, whose engraved stories told tales of past generations, had stone roofs and were built around aqueduct-fed fountains.

Ladies of the Chieftain's extensive family rested on alabaster divans while children played on the stone floor. Overhead, the ever-present banners woven in bold colors fluttered. Potted palms, slaves wielding enormous ostrich feather fans, and urns of sweet pomegranate-based juices added to this relaxing interlude. Anippe found herself easily accepted by these industrious women who worked side by side with the slaves from early light until late morning, returning in the late afternoon to finish the duties assigned to them by the Head-Wife. It pleased Anippe to be spending her days with the smiling children. They showed her their every secret place and shared the stories that their mothers had told them. In this manner, their history passed to new generations.

Occasionally, she was in the presence of Hakeem, though never alone. She wanted to ask him about his father's words, but to speak lightly when little ears could hear was tantamount to shouting from the courtyard. Life here bustled, but there was a formality not present among the nomadic shepherds. Abu Ben Hageed was removed from her circle and never met casually within the compound.

There was a place outside the wall of sand bricks where waste water flowed out of a clay pipe and spilled onto the desert floor. While the elders napped in the heat of the day, the children led Anippe through the gate and to the spillage. She looked at the ground where the children pointed. The sand was discolored from years of receiving the spillage. Hundreds of minute stalks bristled out of the ground.

"What is this?" Anippe asked.

The children hung on to each other, giggling. She smiled back at them.

"I do not see what makes you laugh," she said, stepping towards the sticks.

"No, no," yelped the leader. "Do not go closer. Do not step on them." He ran over to her. "There is nothing there to see."

"I know," said Anippe.

"This is the season. Tomorrow," said the boy, "when the sun is first cresting the horizon, you must look again."

So Anippe waited. As soon as the gates opened, she returned and then stood in awe. Before her on each tiny stem, a blossom had opened, orange, yellow and pale pink. A wave of color stretched away, but as the rising sun touched them, the flowers withdrew, hiding until the next cool dawn. After that, Anippe returned on many mornings to revel in the short burst of beauty. She was always amazed no one else watched the daily birth and death of the desert blooms.

On a particularly warm night, she left the stuffy

confines of her sleeping room, pausing at the archway to the woman's courtyard. Other woman had gathered already, some with fretful children at their breast. Intent on keeping her solitude, Anippe slipped past them and out into the courtyard. Her meandering led her eventually to the well for a cooling sip, after which she sat leaning back against the stone's, intent on the star blazing sky. Overhead, a maelstrom broke, sending flaming stars across the heavens. It was a spectacular sight, holding Anippe's attention until the beating of horses' hoofs was almost upon her.

She peeked above the edge of the well. Across the courtyard, the small gate door was being barred. The rider flung himself off his mount, rushing past towards the Chieftain's quarters. A boy took the reins and led the heavily blowing animal away. Anippe peered intently at the woven saddle with its braiding and tassels. She was sure it was familiar.

"Are you thinking of running off, or perhaps you wish to know more than we are telling you?" The deep voice caught her off guard. Jumping to her feet, she would have darted away, but a strong hand clamped down on her wrist. "Well?"

"No," she whispered. "I came here for quiet meditation. I was startled by the horseman."

Hakeem looked down at her questioningly. His face was in shadows, but his eyes gave off a hard glint. Releasing her, he sighed audibly. "Many nights of late riders come. It is fate that you would be present when this one arrives."

Rubbing her wrist, Anippe looked after the horse. "The horse's trappings are familiar. Ahab-ram had elegant horses. Their saddles and bridles were as beautiful as any woman's robes."

"Your eyes are keen."

"My eyes have protected me in the past."

Hakeem leaned against the well. The wind had risen, tugging at the veils she wore. "The rider did come from Ahab-ram. It will be soon, perhaps, that my father will send for you."

"Will he speak in riddles as he did the last time?"

"It is his way. It is a test to see if you have a mind that thinks or merely nods in agreement."

She moved slowly back towards the woman's

compound. Garbed only in silken trousers that clung to his thighs, the tall man followed.

"I thought much of his words," she said. "I believe he was telling me that there are many who are disquieted by this Pharaoh. A secret Eridinii who wishes to turn back the hourglass. Somehow, they know of my son, though perhaps they don't know where he is. I thought I was alone, but now I believe there are others who follow my fate."

She paused outside the archway. He placed his hands on her shoulders. She knew she should rebuff him, but her knees trembled while her heart warmed at his touch.

"To let in the light, one must open the door," Hakeem whispered. "To unlock the door, we must turn the key. You, my serene beauty, are that key." Kissing her forehead, he left her unable to move as he disappeared into the darkness.

Laying on her pallet, he wondered if his words were a prophesy of her life to come or a declaration from his heart.

CHAPTER 33

When the sun was merely an eyelash's width off the eastern
horizon, Rahaf shook Anippe awake. "Gather your things," she
said. "No longer will you wander with the children. From
today, you will learn what a woman must."

They walked past the groups of matrons, exiting
through a small barred gate hidden behind a pair of plain
columns. A titter ran through the other women as Rahaf and
Anippe advanced.

Beyond the solid wooden door were not the domestic
chores Anippe expected. The air, heavy with an incense of
orange and clove, seemed to hang thickly in the small
enclosure. Perhaps ten young women strolled or reclined in the
center area. Each girl, soon-to-be woman, was followed closely
by a matron swathed in black. Harping voices were followed in

quick order by a change in stance or deportment. Anippe was
to learn a less-then-immediate response brought a vicious
pinch, usually in the tender underarm.

A tall woman who now entered the stoned area must
have been of extreme beauty at one time. Even now, when the
years had drawn harsh fingers across the woman's face,
watchers paused to contemplate the beauty that was still
offered. With skin paler than the lightest sun-bleached desert
sand and eyes the color of bitter chocolate that slanted sharply
upward under thin, artistic brows, she moved towards them as
if gliding on water. Anippe's quick brain recorded all and
more. The small bow-shaped mouth of bright red, the wisdom
and confidence that shone through, and the regal bearing which
encompassed all.

Though she did not bow, Rahaf ducked her head in
respect. Anippe followed suit.

Speaking first to the elder, Rahaf said, "This is Anippe,
Am-Lin, brought to you at my father's command. I have done
as you asked and told her nothing." To Anippe, she added,
"Am-Lin is a rich and well-learned teacher. You will remain

here, in this place, under her care, until she releases you." With another nod, Rahaf was gone.

Am-Lin walked around the younger woman. As a slave, Anippe was used to such scrutiny.

"We will sit," Am-Lin directed. Her hands, which had been clasped within her voluminous sleeves, appeared. It was not the delicate fan of ivory that held Anippe's gaze, but Am-Lin's fingernails. Each one was at least three inches long. Painted with a red lacquer, they had small gems embedded. Her forefingers were covered with a gold shield whose raised design held large rubies.

Tea appeared as opposed to the usual bitter coffee. The serving was china so delicate, Anippe could see the shadow of her fingers through the cup. Am-Lin's servants had the same pale skin and heavily slanted eyes. There had been visitors to thePalace with these same features. Their tongue was a guttural sing-song, impossible to understand.

"You are very old to be here," stated Am-Lin.

Anippe nearly choked on the hot beverage. "I am not old."

"To be just learning to be a woman, you are old."

A girl of perhaps fifteen years glided past, the old woman behind her closely watching each move.

Am-Lin sighed deeply before she continued. Her eloquent mouth leveled out, its outer corners creeping downward.   "This," she said, "is the gatehouse to pleasures. A young girl who is expected to make a good marriage must know many things. Foremost, not to make foolish mistakes. Not only will she manage her husband's home and raise his sons, but she must also make him prideful in the eyes of others. She must know from the onset, though she be a virgin, how to please him, to keep him sated, thereby keeping him agreeable. It is our duty.

"The women who live here do not mix with Chieftain Abu Ben Hakeem's Palace. While you are here, neither will you, nor will you leave until I say. What you learn here is not fodder for idle talk once you are gone. You will be assigned a woman, Zeba, as your first teacher. She is not your friend, but it is required you listen to her carefully." Standing, Am-Lin added, "You are to learn in a few weeks what it takes others at least a year to accomplish. This is Zeba."

Anippe's heart fell. She bit down hard on her tongue so she would not respond to Am-Lin. It was not Ankh's intent to finding a husband nor on being a casual mistress. She had heard of women who taught others the fine points of being coquettish and alluring. Such knowledge was not her desire.

The petite woman who advanced had a sour smell, as if her black cotton shirt and pants had gone unwashed for a long time. Her hair was faded gray, secured in a tight bun on the back of her head. Narrow eyes hidden in heavy folds of skin added nothing to a flat face devoid of color. Am-Lin was well groomed. An expert hand had applied color to her face. The scent of sandalwood and spice swirled around her. Side by side, one was a bright flower, while the other was a rough pebble from the streets.

"Girl," commanded Zeba, issuing the first surprising sharp pinch. Anippe jumped, slapping the withered hand off. But Zeba was ready. A stout cane cracked across Anippe's shoulder. "Listen, girl. You listen to me. It is commanded. You are old; do not be stupid."

Biting her tongue once more, Anippe followed Zeba. They would share a room; meals were shared by all. Anippe would learn to walk, converse, defer to her man in a manner that displayed her to the best advantage, thereby increasing her husband's worth. There was a veiled reference to the lessons that would follow.

"Am-Lin, herself, teaches the use of face colors and scents. You won't have time to learn to play or sing but you will meet daily with Bassin who knows the new Pharaoh's tongue."

Baffled, Anippe turned with a question on her lips, but Zeba's next statement made all clear. "It is said members of Abu Ben Hakeem's household will be moving to the palace." Zeba sniffed. "The only other time you will see Am-Lin is much later when she directs you in the pleasuring arts."

Zeba was nonplussed, but Anippe felt her face redden. It was obvious to her now that Abu Ben Hakeem wanted to make sure she was better armed before she returned to the lion's lair.

Two times the moon grew fat and thin again while

Anippe lived and studied under Zeba's direction. She learned to walk with a smooth step, sit and rise from the floor gracefully, and learned to keep her lips pressed tightly together. There were many times she shook her head at Zeba's warning that a good wife was silent and complacent, but never while Zeba was watching. The only amusement she garnered was when a young man, hooded and naked, was led in. The virgins giggled; they had seen males before, but this was a man! They may have known form, but now they would learn how a man truly worked. The man could not see them, did not know them, but the women learned by touch to tease, leaving a man sighing in pleasure.

Am-Lin arrived wearing a shift of rippling silk and bringing with her an air that inspired awed respect from her students. She directed each girl individually while the others observed. Over a period of two days, they exhausted several young men. Each woman would go to their husband's bed, never having known a man but knowing exactly what a man wanted. Though the younger women would continue to study their arts, Anippe did not have the pleasure of time.

* * *

Am-Lin walked while others still slept. Standing under a scraggly desert palm, Anippe waited until they stood face to face. "It is time for me to leave."

"The gate is open," said Am-Lin. She did not watch the other woman go. She did, however, stand quietly until she heard the wood slide into its frame. Her work, though hurried, was finished.

CHAPTER 34

It had been Anippe's fate in the past to enter the Palace of Pharaoh and escape, but now she knew this would be her last visit. While her heart played at a game of toss with her feelings at this home of her youth, her ever wise head whispered that it was unlikely she would leave alive again.

For Gadi to be able to rise to Pharaoh, Anippe needed to convince the Priests that he was real and worthy. To reach the one Priest who above all others would accept the secret she carried, she needed to discover where he was held prisoner then convince him. This plan discerned by the secret Eridinii of believers had many facets which together would form the glowing puzzle of Egyptian Rule. Only three pieces were given to Anippe: find the Priest, convince the Priest, and if opportunity should present itself, kill Pharaoh. Even as fear froze her heart, she could smile. How would she be able to kill Pharaoh? How would she even get close enough to try?

Her time over the last year had been busy. She had learned the arts of soothsayer, temptress, and warrior. She had been taught about poisons, protocol, and how to tell foe from friend. As before in her life, her head had been , and she was given the short wig of the inner circle, those servants who served the Royal family moving freely throughout the Palace on errands they did not explain to others. At night, she had been instructed to sleep in the woman's dormitory, always on a different pallet. Only by proving to be a friend to the other women could she hope for some clue to learn the whereabouts of Omari. The High Priest to the old Pharaoh was said to have gone violently to his gods. That was a lie. His power was such that none would do more than detain him, keeping him a prisoner far from his people. Pharaoh feared him. Pharaoh's Queen, however, knew more hate than fear.

Anippe's last conversation with Abu Ben Hageed had been exhausting for the old man. He had directed her path, telling her many times that she would be a lone traveler, that if she strayed from the path, she would be lost.

"Do you understand, daughter, that we will not be able to help you? That even though our people will not be far, you will not see them unless you turn against us towards the Devil's Spawn." His rheumy eyes stared unblinking into hers. "Should it appear that your will be frail and fail, your last thought will be the effort of the one who belongs and who is ending your life even if it will cost him his."

"Yes, I understand." Her voice rasped from between dry lips. *Please*, she thought, *do not let the lost life be Hakeem.*

The old man had blessed her, then sent her back to Rahaf. She was allowed two days to rest and meditate, perhaps to sacrifice to her gods in the hopes they would protect her. Then in the darkness, she was awakened to ride among the camel's high bundles of goods again. Once inside the palace walls, she walked with the others into the inner courtyard, then stood as they casually walked away. Rahaf left a light touch on her arm. Hakeem's dark eyes darkened further. There were no words, no promises, no security when the others were gone.

Anippe moved into the mainstream of daily life as

though she had never been elsewhere. Many changes had been made in the palace. Daily she moved to a different place, hiding in the open and acquainting herself with any that would respond. The days were long and information was scarce. Few would even speak of the old Priest; those that did knew little.

"I have heard," said one gossipy slave, pulling water from the stable well, "that he lives near the river. That only the Queen sees him."

"Really?" remarked Anippe, picking up one of the heavy buckets. She knew this already. It had been part of the meager information she had come to the Palace already armed with. "The Queen goes to the river?"

"Unh," was all the response she got.

It had been the advice of Abu Ben Hageed that she stayed away from the inner circle of Pharaoh and his vile Queen, but she had been there many days and had learned nothing. So with the rise of the next sun, she set her steps towards the Palace of the Queen. When she was stopped at the gate, she held up the scrolls she carried in a reed basket. The man stepped aside. Her heart beat heavily in her throat. It was a hard battle not to look back, but she proceeded as though she had a right. Here, too, there had been changes, physical changes to the structure and changes in the decorum of the occupants. The days passed as she learned this new place, arriving with one change of the guards, leaving with another. Eventually, she used different entrances. She wanted to blend in but not be herded with others to a common destination. When she was asked a question or given an order, she lied glibly, then moved away, sometimes even leaving for a day or so.

She knew the women of the new Pharaoh were loud and coarse. So much so that no longer did visiting women stay within these walls, but the children of the wives and consorts did. The main entry, other than at the river level, was actually the second story where the children were. It was a cyclone of screaming babies, shouting nursemaids, and running brats. The next story up was the harem, just as it had been before, but even within those walls, changes had been made. Small rooms had been cut out. Though the walls of lattice patterns offered no privacy, these small oases were greatly coveted. On the fourth and last floor, the Queen's private area, many people resided where few had found residence before. The Queen feared being alone, so she had several women to attend her—physicians, soothsayers, her tailor, bathers, and more.

The oft-desired roof was open to all whenever they desired. It was barren and dusty now. The Queen feared the height and never walked across the hot stones. Some of her women, those from the desert countries, held court there daily. Awnings of silk carried banners identifying the owner. Anippe was surprised at this blatant display. Before the women of Pharaoh lived beneath his banner, one household united.

"Who are you? What do you want?" The eunuch's shrill voice carried across the open space, causing others to turn.

"I was sent with a message for the Queen. I thought to find her here." Anippe stayed her ground, but wondered if this had been a wise move.

Rising from a divan covered by a cloth of pale rose silk, a tall, thin woman approached. Her skin was so black it shone blue. There were raised tattoos on her face, arms, and naked breasts. Silken scarfs of reds, yellows, and purples wound around her. The woman towered above Anippe. Struck by the beauty of this willowy woman, Anippe forgot to bow. She felt the sharp rap of the eunuch's cane.

"Do you not know your place?" He hissed.

"I am sorry, Great One." Sweat gathered on her flesh and she gulped for air. Had she just destroyed everything? "I-I was so blinded by your beauty I became as stone." Reaching out towards the woman's foot, Anippe was contrite. She had been raised to regard the royalty as Gods-On-Earth. Her movements were sincere, there was no need for her to act.

The woman drew up taller. "Go. The Queen does not come here. Her stomach will not allow it." Watching Anippe crawl backward, the tall woman called out, "Wait. What is the message? Perhaps I will take it to her."

With her face pressed against the dusty stone, Anippe spoke of a new apprentice for the tailor. There was no answer. Daring to raise her eyes several minutes later, she found herself alone and scuttled away. She would never return to the rooftop.

There were also other places Anippe did not go, the Queen's chambers, the room of the tailor, and near the children.

She passed among them when needed but, just as did the wives and concubines, she tried to avoid them. The previously hidden staircase she had used after the slaughter had been discovered during the renovations. It was heavily guarded now. She had never seen so many servants in the palace, yet they all had one common agenda. When they could escape their duties, the slaves and eunuchs moved into the wide stone corridor, away from their harping mistresses. Since the coming of Queen Kanika, this area that had at one time been merely a road from here to there had taken on the aspects of a marketplace. Soothsayers held court. Trinket sellers offered their wares. There was fancy stitching offered, and even trays of sweets, all harked by the owner in hope that some wife or maid servant would buy. Seated on benches or hurrying down the slave corridor, servants, free and slave, chatted with each other, relieved to be free of their burdens. The guards did not admonish them and there seemed to be no Domo there to keep order. This great change worked in Anippe's favor.

It did not take a wise eye to judge which wives or concubines were poor or not highly regarded. Their clothing was older, shabbier, and perhaps passed off by another. Often they were doing for themselves that which a slave should do. The women of power had not only their own servants but were inventive in keeping the common slaves busy. Small cliques did not exist here, but larger entourages did.

Taking a basket of stitching, Anippe sat on a small stool. Stone lattice allowed her to hear but not be seen. Before her, a fountain of green and cream-colored stone babbled. A quarter-way past, along the fountain, a soothsayer held court on a faded prayer rug. Old, dusty robes were merely a camouflage, Anippe knew, for this woman was here daily in the same spot. No other tried to stake a claim to the area. Many soothsayers spread throughout the corridors and in the gardens, but this one seemed to draw many of the women of Pharaoh.

It is best, Anippe thought, *to avoid the rich and mighty who would have a soothsayer brought to them.*

But she had been wrong, for the woman of Pharaoh Manu took the liberty to move about the enormous building freely. Where women of the old Pharaoh had shopkeepers, soothsayers, and seers brought to them, these women traveled down the long corridor and into the gardens to seek their favorites. The entire Palace was a stage on which they could strut and flaunt their wares.

They were so brazen, so fearless that many traveled without their accompanying slaves in tow. Behind the lattice, a particularly busy seer knelt. Her clientele threw their offering in a crumbled brass pot and waited. The haughty stood unafraid of who would hear while others sat close, leaning hungrily towards the toothless witch. Anippe listened.

Today, the clink of clay coin against metal caught her attention. A woman knelt before the cross-legged crone while an errant breeze tugged at her sheer veiling. Watching in amazement, Anippe saw the crone reach into the pot to retrieve the offering. The old woman rubbed the coin, her mouth curving slightly downward. Her customer, though of a higher rank, boasted few jewels and her offering was meager.

Anippe could see the crone's thoughts in the furrowed brow. Anippe smiled. She thinks it best to get past this small crocodile before the larger ones come to feed.

The mystic threw her bones and dice. "I see. I see."

There were no theatrics, no moaning, no weaving, no clutching of her chest.

"Yes," whispered the customer, handsome and fine-boned, but not pretty.

"You are looking for a child. You are waiting to be called to the attention of Pharaoh. He does not see you."

The customer gasped. Her hand covered her mouth, her eyes, and then her mouth again. The soothsayer had all the information she needed. This lesser tribute of some small nation had been here a long time and would probably never be taken to spend the night with Pharaoh.

"Only when the Ba of the Queen boards the Mesektet Boat and moves down the River of Death will your star rise." The crones chin fell to her chest. With an effort, she roused herself. "Did a message come?" she asked the pharaoh's woman, her voice falsely weak and faltering.

The customer had already risen and was moving quickly away. Holding her veil over her face, she could hide her eyes, but not the sound of her sobs. Again, the crone fished the coin out, then hid it away in her heavy robes. A different woman, bejeweled and well fed, approached, and the crone smiled.

For the rest of the day, Anippe sat and listened. During the time she employed this tactic, she learned more about the inhabitants than in all the while she had been here. Abu Ben Hageed warned her to know well her enemies. She listened, repeating in her mind what she heard so she would not forget.

When the sun rose to its zenith the next day and most looked for a place to rest, Anippe rose from the bench, hiding her wig in the basket. With a bone needle, she scraped her inner arm above the elbow. Careful not to draw blood, the scrape was enough to leave a bright red mark. With just as much care, she entered the harem. On the far side of the bathing rooms, she saw the lowly wife. Still caught in sadness, the woman's eyes were dull. She wore the rumbled robes of the previous day.

Kneeling, Anippe noted the catches in the fabric and the broken stitches in the embroidery along the edging. Mending had probably been done by this same woman.

"Great Lady," said Anippe.

After a moment, the eyes flicked towards her.

"Are you speaking to me?" The woman's voice was a husky whisper, the effect of hours spent crying in despair.

"Yes, Great Lady. I have come because I need your help."

The woman searched around for the perpetrator of this farce. "Why would you come to me? Go away," she said.

Anippe held her ground. This was a scene from her own life; she knew how it would be played. "No, please. Last night I had a dream. I saw a woman, the face of a woman, who could help me." She drew back slightly but still spoke in a low voice. "I am a seer, and know many things, but one such as myself has harmed me. I need a pure spirit to cleanse my wound."

"You are a soothsayer?" Distrust still shone in the woman's dark eyes. "And you cannot heal yourself?"

"When one seer casts the black dust against another, only a pure light can stop the rot of death. I asked my gods for a light. I was offered you." Anippe's mouth was dry. The woman did not seem to understand. Anippe got bolder. "I have always sat in the garden under the olive tree. A few days ago, I ventured within the palace walls. I found a beautiful fountain of soft green and white. In my mind, I saw a smiling face and thought this was a place for me, but an evil witch came. She wore robes of blood red and black. She smelt of old oil and rot. Her skin was pitted with many black marks. Her mouth, a gaping black hole." It was a very accurate description of the crone.

The woman sat up, her eyes wide and mouth open. "What happened?"

"She screamed at me. She pinched me and hit me. When I tried to escape, she reached out and clawed me." Anippe held up her arm in evidence. "Now I can feel her evil there. I need one of pure light to touch it to run the evil away." Falling all the way to the floor, Anippe touched the woman's robe. "I do not have much, and cannot offer money. I can only give what I have. Your future."

"I know my future," said the woman, her voice flat.

"No, your future has a thread which needs to be woven to change it."

"A thread? A change? You know this?"

"It came to me in my dream," said Anippe.

"What do you need from me?" asked the woman.

"Great Lady, Pure Light. I need you only to touch my wound." When the woman reached out, Anippe pulled her arm back. "You must be sure; you must see the healing in your heart, for if you do not I will surely die."

The woman nodded and extended her hand again. This time, Anippe allowed the other to touch her arm. With a gasp, Anippe fell to the floor, obviously in a faint. Having positioned herself on the outer side of the wife's couch, Anippe knew no one would see her charade and question it. The wife responded exactly as hoped, jumping up to kneel beside her. Anippe's eyelids fluttered; she moaned.

"Are you all right? Should I call a physician?"

"No, no, Pure Light, I will be well. It was just a shock." Pushing herself up on to her elbows, Anippe gazed wonderingly at her savior.

"Meya. I am Meya," said the wife.

"Ah, you are more. You are wife to Pharaoh, The Great

Light."

"There are concubines greater than I." Rising to her feet, Meya moved back.

"Princess, I owe you my life and I will give payment as I have promised." From her basket, Anippe withdrew a set of bone dice and some bone chips that she and Rahaf had collected. Giggling, they had selected those that looked interesting. With great ceremony, she wiped clean a space on the floor. "Wave your hand over these offerings so they will know to do your bidding." Instructed Anippe.

Meya passed her hand over the collection. Rocking back and forth with her eyes closed, Anippe shook the dice in her cupped hands, mumbling in a barely audible voice. Dropping them to the floor, she bent over them, moving her hands about. "They say..." she said.

"Yes?"

"...you must weave a thread. That to do so you must thread a needle."

"A needle?" Meya sat back, frowning.

"Yes," said Anippe. She continued to rock, waving her

hands gently. When Meya frowned, Anippe continued, hoping the other woman would catch on by herself. It was not to be. "The thread is your knowledge. The needle is the Queen."

With a bitter laugh, Meya pointed her foot at the dice. "You have wasted your payment. The Queen does not know I exist." She moved to go; the threat of tears darkening her eyes.

"You will best yourself by waiting until the Queen goes to bathe. You will not allow yourself to be deterred, but will present yourself, telling her you know of a theft. A theft of her own possessions."

"I know of no theft," said Meya, suspiciously.

"Ah, but you do," Anippe said. Sitting back, she continued. "In the days past, you walked through the corridor. You had been to a seer. As you left, another approached; she offered a bauble to the seer, a ringlet stolen from the Queen."

"I did not see that."

"You were there. You saw the other, did you not? Do you remember the offering?"

Meya thought hard. She remembered the seer and her hateful words. She remembered passing the other woman.

There was no way she could have heard the woman sneer to her servant that the Queen would never miss the ringlet, though Anippe hidden in the alcove had. When Meya turned to Anippe, she found the other gone.

Days passed. Anippe wandered the other paths of the great Palace grounds along the river, searching for information. Which is why she found herself when a death barge crossed to the other side. There were many Priests, slaves, and mourners. This was the burial procession of someone of rank. Joining a small group of on-lookers, she inquired about the personage.

"It is one of the wives of Pharaoh." she was told. "It is not a good thing."

"Why not?" Anippe asked.

"The woman was a thief. She crossed the Queen and was killed."

"Yes," said another, "and a false seer as well."

The hairs on Anippe's arm raised as the group dispersed. She moved quickly towards the harem's garden. Her ruse allowed her back through the guarded gates. A guard watched her go. He had seen her many times in different places and she was familiar to him. He watched her walk away.

It did not take long for Meya, who was wearing a new robe of saffron-colored silk, to find her. A slave followed closely.

"I have looked for you," said Meya.

"I have been here, Princess."

"Yes, of course." Meya spoke in a rush. "I did as you said, as the prophesy told. You were right. The Queen was so angry." Meya trembled. "I thought I would die, but she protected me, gifted me."

Smoothing her new robe, she knelt before Anippe while her slave dropped coins into the reed basket. "Tell me."

"A prophesy is not for idle ears," Anippe said.

Meya waved the slave away, sighing, "She will go back to her duties. I only took her today because she was idle at that moment and I could. Now tell me."

Slowly sorting through her basket, Anippe waited until no one was near. "It would not do well, Princess, for all to know whence you gain insight."

"I told no one." Meya blushed, "I was going to, but

everything happened so fast. Then the Queen gave me this new robe, and it was just... just too late." Her eyes were still downcast, her ears a dark, molten red.

Gently, Anippe raised the other woman's face, cool fingers beneath a hot chin. "I am concerned," Anippe said in a soft tone, "lest someone think you are evil or worse and cast against you. I would not wish to see you harmed because your needs caused you to not be prudent. It takes long hours to weave a good cloth, to stitch a beautiful garment."

"I know," said the other.

Once again, Anippe bent over the bones. Carefully following the pattern she had set forth. Many of those seeking soothsayers and seers were ruled by superstition. When a tradition was established, it must be followed. In the midst of her mumbling, she jumped back, stumbling to her feet.

When Meya cried out in alarm, Anippe hastened back to her place. "I am sorry to frighten you, Princess. It just came so fast, the scene, the evil."

"Evil?" Meya questioned.

"Yes, I see it clearly. You will be in a place of water,

wet with great scents of far places. You will see an evil that

slithers hidden from others and sound the alarm, saving many."

Panting, she ran her hand over her eyes, then scooped up the

bones.

"What?" Meya's eyes were large. "What?"

"There is no more."

"What evil, what water?" Meya shook Anippe.

"Was there a prophesy?" asked Anippe, rousing as she

had seen the other seer do, but Meya jumped to her feet and ran

away.

So it was in the early dawn when Anippe took up the

pointed stick and a sack of the snake catchers and hunted. In

the area where the man-made lake had once stood, final

construction was being made to a large dormitory that would

house the overflow of Pharaoh's women. Where others before

him had kept large harems, Manu's women numbered, as did

the populace of small villages. Over 400 wives and concubines

lived beneath Pharaoh's banner. Few he had chosen; most were

a gift of state. At this time, he had 257 children, which he often

pitted against each other or used as payment for commerce.

They, as most of his women, were rarely seen and never considered. Only his Queen warranted his attention because she and she alone participated in his every perversion. What evil he did not think of, she did. Together they constituted a power which made even the underworld shudder.

This was the fearful tale Abu Ben Hageed had whispered to Anippe. She kept it closed in her mind, opening it only when she felt herself becoming too complacent.

Among the huge stones, tackles, and weight were many hidden crevices cool in the heat of day. Workers had been bitten recently and died while their brothers continued to sweat beside them. Danger lurked in the cool shadows. Scuttling her stick beneath a block, leaning still slightly raised, Anippe flushed out a small snake. Its length was barely that of her forearm, but its fangs could kill even the elephants in Pharaoh's paddocks. Deftly the young woman pinned the reptile against the sand, then she pinched it tightly just beyond its jaws before she lifted it. The writhing body wrapped around her wrist, flayed away, and wrapped again. Carefully, she dropped it into her sack, twisting and tying in one motion.

Once it was hidden inside her basket, she looked about her. There could be no witnesses. Sweat covered her body. She remembered the first time she had seen a snake kill, and that fear returned.

She left the snake in the sack for three days, needing it to be weak. Every day she sat in the garden, casting lots and waiting.

Finally, Meya returned. Though she still wore her new robe, her face was downcast and grim.

"I have thought much of what you said when I was here last," she said. "I have watched but seen nothing."

Anippe gazed upward, running her hands across her eyes and along her face. Meya gazed upward also, obviously wondering what might be there.

"This would be a good day to lounge in the scented waters," Anippe said.

Meya nodded, still intent on the bones laying idle in the other's lap. Taking up the bones, Anippe rattled them in her hands. Meya could not raise her eyes from the clatter.

"Many will rest there today, eating, drinking, gossiping

like shopkeepers."

Meya was almost panting. Anippe threw the bones. For a long while, both women bent forward, one setting the bait while the other circled the offering.

Raising her mumbling voice, Anippe whispered. "Look. Look here, see the death, see the deadly line sliding towards the innocent. Oh, they are lost for sure. Too bad. Too bad. No, wait, what is this? There you are, yes, it is the same as the line on your hand. You have come to save them all and glory shall be offered to you. The same line I tell you, the same line."

"What line?" Meya inspected her palm.

In her hurry to point it out, Anippe, seemingly innocently, erased the line etched in the sand. Meya was covered with dust. Anippe, who had feared Meya would not understand and therefore not go to the baths, had made sure the girl sat downwind of her. Throughout the whole exchange, Anippe would lift a fistful of fine sand then allow it to slide between her fingers. Dust borne on the wind drifted to Meya, settling on her face, her hair, her pretty yellow robe. Though

Meya ran her hands repeatedly over her face, tendrils of dust, like a spider's web, remained. Not used to sitting for a long period in the sun, Meya, whose skin was fairer than Anippe's, bore beads and rivulets of sweat, keeping the fine grains of sand attached to her. Though it was not becoming, she itched, scratched, and repeatedly wiped at the irritant.

Finally, Anippe closed their meeting. "Even in the clean waters, free of all worry, one must be vigilant," she said.

"Yes," Meya agreed. "Cool, clean water."

When Anippe entered the Queen's Palace, she moved with a determined step towards the area where the harem's bath was. She would not enter, but sat beyond the heavy lattice wall, stitching and listening. When she heard the tinkle of Meya's voice beyond, Anippe rose. Now true danger entered her ruse. She watched closely the servants and slaves who passed the guards to enter the baths. Prior to that day, Anippe had identified a few who might accept her offer and aid her ruse. Removing her wig to better become of no description, she approached a free woman heavy with child. The woman carried a large basket of salt water sponges freshly cleaned and dried. Stopping the woman before she was within sight of the guards, Anippe was brief. She held in her hand the gold trinket, the ram's head, she had found so long ago when it had fallen from the head of Pharaoh's son.

"This is yours to keep. More than you will see in all the years you have fingers. Only this you will do for it; take this bag, carefully, loosen the tie and drop it where Princess Meya will espy it. Do you know her? Good. Do not be seen, do not tarry."

The lure of gold was more than the woman, whose own children starved as the harem women wasted, could pass up. She made room under the sponges, tucked the gold in her cheek, and hurried away, as did Anippe. It would not be good to be found in this place if the woman cheated on their deal.

Clenching her teeth while her stomach writhed, Anippe ran. She had taken a great chance. Finally, she stopped where others worked and took a short broom and bent from the waist, swept the sands of Egypt from the Palace of Pharaoh. She did not know that the woman plucked at the tie, dropped the bag on the damp tiles near the edge of the sunken pool then offered her sponges in a voice cracked and fearful that shrilled on Meya's nerves, causing her to look up from her lounging water seat. It was not Meya that first saw the asp, thirsty and hungry, slither from the dryness of the sacking but, when the slave woman screamed, it was Meya that screeched like the devil winds of a desert storm, pointing and ordering everyone away. If the sacking was noticed, it was not mentioned. The free woman, slaves and harem occupants all ran from the area as the guards thundered in to beat life from the reptile.

Though she shivered in fear, Meya accepted the accolades of the other women and the recognition of Queen Kanika. Her status had changed.

CHAPTER 35

Meya was not the only one to feel the tight, crushing grip of fear. In the night, laying on her thin pallet of straw, Anippe's sleep was crowded with hitherto unknown specters. She dreamed of walking through the gardens of the Palace, the heady scent of large colorful flowers surrounding her. She was of unease. Her bowels pained her, causing cramps that sent her to her knees, but she dared not crouch over a cess-pot. Sleeping within her was a slim, oily serpent. As long as it slept, she was safe but, should she try to press it from her body, it would awaken and kill her.

When she finally struggled awake, terror held sleep at bay. After a short while, she left her bed and wandered until she found herself in a stone enclosure with a floor of sand. She sat, casually drawing pictures of the oasis in the fine dust. Pictures which the Priests of Pharaoh Eridinii could have used to find her son, Gadi. The only threat to Pharaoh, one that needed to be destroyed.

Outside the Palace walls, far from the center of the city, in a place where within two rooms three families crowded. A woman who had married into this family, the woman Anippe had chosen to fulfill her plan, also lay awake in fear. Poor and hungry her whole life, she lay beside her husband, surrounded by her three children, while a fourth grew large in her belly. Already the eldest two, barely more than toddlers, spent their days running threads for their uncle, the rug weaver.

Today, the woman had been given a golden gift. She had taken it with no thought. Now she regretted the incident. She did not regret the gold, but she was terrorized by the memory of what had occurred afterward. How could they, her husband and herself, explain this wealth? She did not know who they could trust, and she did not know how to tell her husband, a captain in the Queen's guard, what she had done.

CHAPTER 36

Daily, Anippe waited for Meya, some days in the garden, some days in the great hall, or among the fountains. Meya would always search her out. When Meya, irritated, demanded to know why among all the soothsayers, Anippe roved from place to place. Anippe was prepared with a ready answer.

"Just as the winds move from here to beyond, so do the spirit guides who provide me with the answers to your questions. It is not my place to demand they come to me, but rather my respect that takes me to them."

Wide eyed, Meya nodded solemnly. "Do they speak to you today? Do they tell you if I will soon know Pharaoh?" It was the same question she asked every day.

Anippe was hard pressed to evade an answer. She had cultivated Meya to obtain information regarding the old High

Priest that only Queen Kanika visited, but Meya had proven to be a useless tool. She did not pay attention to events within the harem, then eagerly gossip about them as others did. It was in this manner Anippe garnered her information, listening, eavesdropping on others. If a conversation did not involve an appearance of Pharaoh, Meya was not interested. Indeed, Anippe considered Meya the shallowest person she had ever encountered.

It was on this day, while Anippe remained kneeling on her rug after Meya left and feeling unsure how to proceed, that she was approached by three giggling girls who were concubines. Given as tribute to Pharaoh, the three sisters so closely resembled each other that Anippe called them merely One, Two, and Three.

"Ha, we found you," giggled One.

"Yes. She thought she was sly, but she's not as smart as we," giggled Two. Three merely nodded.

Anippe smiled. "You found me? You were looking for me? Why would you search me out?"

In their giggly, light-aired way, the three told Anippe

their story. How they had been given by their father to the legend of Pharaoh, how they were considered an oddity by the Queen, three children of one birth. She allowed them to live unfettered here instead of in a far-off Palace or dormitory. Finally, they spoke of Meya and her extraordinary gift.

"I heard her, after she found the asp and battled it to death, tell another that her seer had said she would overcome a poisoned monster," said One. The others nodded in ascent. "It was a huge snake; it could have easily swallowed a person whole."

Anippe blinked. "Did you see it?"

"No," said Three with a shudder. The girls huddled closer.

"Ah, so Meya spoke of her seer?"

"Yes, we asked her who you were, but she would not tell us," said One.

"But we followed her," said Three.

"We have money to pay," said Two. The three girls offered their clay coins, more than Meya ever appeared to have. Anippe selected only a few before proceeding to provide a spectacular performance that left the three young girls panting.

Surely, Anippe thought, these three prepubescent children would have little to offer besides the occasional coins and entertainment.

It was on this day also, almost at the edge of the night, that Anippe sat alone on a stone bench in the slave feeding area, her half portion of mash forgotten in her lap.

"If that bowl falls to the ground and breaks, you will be hungry this night," said a deep voice beside her.

Her head snapped around. Hakeem was here! His eyes glittered with laughter.

"Ah, ah, stay seated, eat your meal. We do not want others to see us." He focused on his own bowl, but his eyes slid over her.

"I am so glad to see you," Anippe said. Her head was also bowed, but her ears blushed red. An excited tension rolled through her body. If someone else had come to sit near, they would have felt it, also. She wondered how he had found her.

"I have seen you and watched unknown many times."

Hakeem said.

"You have?"

"Do not look at me or I will not be able to do this again. I take a risk now that my father would not like."

A woman passed before them.

"We go," Rahaf whispered without stopping. He was gone. Anippe did not dare look up to watch him go. She knew her heart would show in her eyes.

From then on, her resolve had strengthened. She'd become again as sly as a cat on the prowl.

* * *

One, Two and Three, returned almost as often as Meya. Their visits were much more entertaining, however. It was less than the cycle of the moon when they approached Anippe in the Hall of Fountains. She was hidden among the lattice work, idly working at nothing but cocooned in the short conversation she had had with Hakeem the night before. Thrice he had appeared during the evening meal. Each meeting was sweeter than the last, though none had lasted more than moments.

Normally the stronger, the girl Anippe called One, was

supported this time by her sisters. Her flat chested body heaved with sobs she tried to smother behind her hands.

"Please," entreated her sisters, "lift the curse that befalls us."

"Tell me of what you speak." Anippe looked cautiously around, fearful of others who would eavesdrop on her.

With the prodding of her sisters, One said, "He looked right at me, his eyes into my eyes. He spoke without words. I am doomed to a painful death."

Dissolving into tears, she threw herself across the dicing field into Anippe's lap. Rather than push her away, the older woman pulled the child closer, offering the comfort of her arms. Two and Three moved without invitation into the same embrace. In whispering voices, they gave forth much Anippe wished to know.

It was as Anippe had heard. Kanika did indeed visit the ousted Priest Omari, but he was not housed somewhere in the city or deep within a temple. He was held on a barge that floated the river Nile day in and day out. The only time the barge touched land was when it was called by a brass horn to the steps on the river's edge of the Queen's Palace.

"That's why no one is allowed to go there anymore," said Two.

"But no one talks of this," Anippe said. She was suspicious of knowledge these three children would have that others did not.

Separating themselves only slightly from her, three pairs of identical eyes met hers. "There is a reason we tell no one. We have decided to tell you only if you promise to lift the curse."

Anippe angled herself to be able to see if anyone approached. "Speak softly. I will help you, but I need to know what you carry in your heart." She handed each girl a bone to hold as a talisman to protect them.

"We came here when we were small children. We are sisters of the same birth. An oddity in our land." One spoke, the others nodded. "Though we were a gift to Pharaoh, it was his Queen who took us. She said that Ra had told her to look for us, we would help her in silence."

"It was fearful," said Two, "when she and her Priests

took our blood and swore us to fidelity. We have never before spoken of this, even among ourselves."

"But when we went to the Priest about the curse, he sent us away," said One.

"He would not even listen," said Three.

"So, you came to me and you are sure you will tell me all?"

"I dreamed of you last night. I know you were sent to help me," One said. Her tears were gone and resolve shone from her dark chocolate eyes.

"Continue."

"After we had been inducted into Queen Kanika's inner circle, we found others so sworn. Most are slaves who have been altered to make them worthy."

"They are kept separate from all others. There is a small room in her apartment where they live."

"They have no tongues. They do not speak."

"And no one sees them?" Anippe asked.

"Yes, everyone sees them. But they are also the slaves that accompany the Queen to her bath. She will not bathe while any others are present, nor use the slaves everyone else does."

"These slaves actually have two functions? How many are there?"

"Four."

"Almost every day, when the sun is hottest and others rest, a there is the sound of a horn calling into the wind. It comes from above on the Palace rooftop. Most think it is a call to rest, but it actually calls the barge."

"If the timing is erratic, why hasn't someone noticed?"

"To whom?" asked Three. "Who would question the Queen as to when she had the horn sounded?"

It was a viable question.

"It is at this time we accompany the Queen and her slaves. We carry baskets of food and offerings. We go onto the barge, no one comes off. It stays until the Queen is done."

"How do you get to that place unseen?"

"There is a hidden staircase in the Queen's chamber. It comes out behind her altar. A stone moves," Two said.

"You have seen this, Priest?"

"Yes." In voices barely above a whisper, they spoke of

a very old man who wore spectacular copper headdresses, of incense, and demands the Queen made, but the elder did not provide. "She is looking for a child."

"A boy."

"He is of another."

"What else do you know about this child? Another what?" Anippe's throat was dry, her stomach clenched.

"We know nothing else of the child."

"Tell me about the barge."

"It is large, rich looking, not like her other. There are soldiers who look like oarsman but who have weapons at their feet."

"None have tongues."

"And none of the slaves have eyes."

"What?"

"No," One looked at Three, "the helmsman has both eyes and tongue."

"Yes," Two agreed.

"Alright," Anippe said, "it's a large, noble barge. With hidden soldiers, who cannot speak and never get off the barge.

Slaves who do not speak or see and never get off the barge, but a helmsman who can both see and speak but never leaves the barge. How do you know this?"

Two giggled, "We can see, we can speak, and we can hear."

"How many people are on the barge?"

"Many, the count of all our hands."

Anippe's skin prickled. "Where do they get supplies, food, cooking fuel, whatever they need?"

"That's what we give them."

Anippe needed to think. "I am going to make you a talisman," she said to One. "Tomorrow you return here and I will give it to you. It will protect you always." She waved her hands over the girl, mumbling while she pinched the child's cheeks and arms. After the girls left, she folded her rug into her basket.

The highest building overlooking the river was the Temple to Ra, reaching towards the sun, tall and narrow. The temple was outside the palace walls but an enclosed corridor provided a way for slaves or palace occupants to move between the two. Anippe climbed the steep steps to the place of offering. From this point, she could look down upon the river. There were many vessels of various sizes and ornamentation floating up and down or even across. She could see some carried supplies to the city or people and stopped at any of a number of docks. Then there were those used only for the pleasures of the upper caste. Later, when she spoke idly to a ferry man whose responsibility was the efficient transfer of Pharaoh's soldiers, she leaned that few of the larger barges never docked for any length of time.

"It is safer," he said, "to row aimlessly on the river, then be battered against the shore." The man also showed her how to tell the owner of one barge from another using the banner flags that flew from the great curved neck of the vessels.

In the gathering dusk, Anippe stitched a simple amulet bag, then filled it with a small amount of sand, some hair, and the jawbone of a fish. If the chattering trio dared look inside, they would have no guess about the contents. While she worked, she watched the river men toil against Mother Nile.

No message showed itself, no knowledge was gleaned.

Days passed as she pried what she could from the sisters. It was slow work; there was always the chance they would question her interest. Meya still appeared every few days, but the gossip she brought was not linked to Anippe's need. Still, Anippe tucked each tidbit away.

CHAPTER 37

Sunrise had been hot and surly. Pendents hung limply from their staffs. Even the act of chewing the flat bread and boiled mash caused sweat to rise. In the relative coolness of the stone corridor, Anippe stood among the perpetual foot traffic that catered to the Royals while a multitude of harem occupants filed past. On the river side, the wide access staircase was open to all. This morning, the River Pavilion was open! Following the women, selected children and slaves were the soothsayers and trinket sellers who could pay the bribe.

Anippe joined the flow. She had forgotten how enormous the pavilion was. Wide, shallow white marble brought from afar created a fan-shaped staircase that led down to the very height of the river. The pavilion, with its thick stone columns, so wide six women could not join hands around one, was decorated in shades of blue and green stone against white. It was cool and inviting. Long, sheer panels hung from overhead, waving in the breeze that traveled only along the water. They created the illusion of privacy in this vast cavern.

Already most of the hard stone benches were taken. Slaves carried pillows, rugs, treats for their mistresses. There was much chatter now as each set up their small court; later the children would leave and it would quieten. The girl moved across the floor, her sandals smacking the floor lightly. At the far edge, more steps dropped into the actual river. Beaters smacked the water with long paddles to discourage crocodiles from entering. Lush reeds grew right to the edge of the steps. Children played in the water while nurses held on to them with silken ropes. When they were through, the women would wander into the shallow edges, either in short tunics or with their hems tied up around their waists. Anippe breathed in the smell of the river, the wet mud, sweetness and stink. It was all good.

"Huh? What are you about, girl?" Loust, Pharaoh's Major Domo, stood behind her. Anippe felt her knees tremble.

She had not seen him in years, but she knew him immediately. He had come here this day to verify his appointee did as he was told regarding oversight of the Queen's Palace.

"Master," she squeaked, falling to her knees.

"Master Loust has asked you a question, stupid girl." The Queen's Domo's voice sounded as squeaky as hers. Though he may reign here, he still answered to Loust.

"I-I go for figs." Anippe stammered.

"Here?" asked Loust.

"No, no, I was tempted. The mother river calls," she said, then gasped in pain as the Domo's cane came down across her back.

Jumping to her feet, she hurried away in the direction he pointed. After that, she took up a basket of fruit, passing from one wife to another and avoiding the Domo throughout the day even after Loust left. She espied Meya reclining along the outside edge, away from the coolness of the river, but she did not see the triplets. Though she spent the time looking for a place to secret herself, she found none. The only items that did not come and go with the women were the columns and the stone benches. These were merely flat stone tables set on two oval columns. There was no way to hide unseen under them.

Shortly after high sun, the big copper horns sounded. Everyone immediately moved towards the staircase. Sullen faces and harsh words showed the displeasure of the court women forced to leave this comfort. Among them, slaves rushed about, collecting everything that had been brought and escaping just as the great gates clanged together. Guards took up their post; assistants to the Domo made one final sweep to verify the pavilion was once again deserted.

Along with all others, Anippe had been ushered out. Today, she did not find a place to sit but went instead to the offering site in the temple tower. The stone was hot to touch and her hurried climb to the top left her feeling vaguely ill and faint. She had barely arrived when the horn sounded again, a different tone, the call to rest, or so she had previously thought.

Shading her eyes, she watched. Minutes passed, as did the flotilla. Finally, one barge broke ranks. With strong sweeps of the oars, it pulled into the pavilion area. She could see only the outer edge, which remained there before pulling back out into the river traffic. Other boats made way. Now she could see

several people in white moving about on the deck. These must

be the muted slaves and One, Two, and Three. The barge

moved away from her. She thought to leave this place, hot as

Hades, but decided instead to lean into the small shadow

provided and wait.

The wait was long. Sure that the sundial would have

moved to the next raised digit, Anippe pulled herself out of her

stupor when the barge, this time riding the current, reappeared.

She noted the flag of gold on green with two black stripes. The

edging of the barge was painted the same green and gold with

black diagonal striping every few yards. The illusion of

grandeur, with no ownership. On legs of straw, she climbed

down, her head bursting with questions and the pain caused by

the cruel sun. Ra would make her pay for what she wished to

know.

There were rumors Pharaoh and his family would soon

be traveling to the summer palace. There was no way Anippe

would be able to follow.

When the River Pavilion gates were opened again a few

days later, she followed her former ruse but, when all were called away, she melted into the water and hid in the rushes, waiting. The beaters were gone; she dared not leave the water but worried about the river monsters. Unable to stop fear from clattering her teeth together, she sat in the muck, rubbing her arms and hoping for courage. At last, the barge approached.

It was as the girls had said. The barge pulled in and slaves hefted the Queen aboard, then loaded all they had brought. The barge and all its occupants, old and new, pulled out. Anippe climbed out of the water, sitting on the step nearest the rushes, waiting again. When the barge returned, she stepped into the rushes and moved deeper in the water. Standing as tall as she dared, she reached for a line that dangled near the stern. A quick look showed the Queen's entourage hurrying across the blue and green tiles.

When the boat came about, Anippe grasped the line. Immediately she was yanked off her feet, bumped against the bottom of the craft, and presented with a clear view of the large, dangerous rudder. Forgotten were the evils of the river, as the danger of the barge presented themselves. Hand over hand, she pulled herself away from the back of the boat and close to the hull itself. She could hear the oarsman grunting. When they were caught in the current again, the oars were pulled to rest; the river was all the power needed. In the design of the boat was a small shelf just below where the oars dipped from the oar holes. With much effort, Anippe pulled herself onto the ledge, then crept up to where she would be hidden from the view of others by the shadow of the oars.

At last darkness fell. They were far from the city. A heavy splash signaled the dropping of an anchor. The barge swung around until its weight was caught. Now Anippe was on the off-shore side. She was barely able to grasp the edge of an oar, preventing herself from being thrown into the river. Sure that she had been told the boat would not halt its continuous journey back and forth, she shivered in fear. In the darkness, she could hear smaller boats come alongside. Men clamored into them, but none climbed back onto the barge. She waited.

When she heard no sounds save occasional snoring, she climbed over the oar, squeezing beside it and through the oar hole. There was no one there. A guard moved past to the back of the boat, dipping his cup into a smoldering pot. He sat against the hull, chewing noisily. She had no idea where to go. On the breeze, she could smell the boiled meat and then just a quick waft of pipe smoke. She crawled forward. In a heavy chair, a man sat alone, gazing over the land. He had a long narrow clay pipe in his hand from which tendrils of smoke floated. Anippe moved backwards. A bright shaft of moonlight caused her to halt. She was afraid of being seen.

The same beam caught a clumsy shape beside the chair, throwing a bright beam on burnished metal. It was a hat, a crown, tall and ornate. Was this perhaps the Priest she had searched for? Crawling closer, she tried to see him. The area surrounding him was open; anyone there would be in clear view. She crawled forward until she was in the shadow cast by the chair. Pulling her legs up, she whispered through the reed and wood, "Father?"

"What? Who is there?"

"Please do not give me away." She begged. "Only tell me your name."

"I am High Priest Omari, Counsel to Pharaoh Seth, the

one, true ruler of Egypt," he said loudly.

"*Shhh*," she whispered. "Do you not know he is dead?"

The old man lowered his voice. "What do you want? Who are you?"

"I have little time. Why are you held here?"

In a whisper, Omari told of his capture, that the new Pharaoh feared him, and of his long time of imprisonment. He had been trapped in this floating jail for over a year. "They do not dare destroy me, for they believe I know the source of a secret they seek. Another who thought to save himself spoke of it, but after much torture, they killed him."

"Sibes," Anippe said.

The old man started for the first time. "How do you know his name?"

"And the secret is a son, a son of Seth, who escaped the slaughter."

"How do you know this?" Omari's voice was rising.

"Quietly, Old Father," Anippe said. "It is not a son of Seth they actually seek, but rather the secret child of Kaakhsi, born to him by a free woman."

"No," Omari corrected. "A slave."

"You are wrong, Reverend Father, a free woman. This free woman."

There was silence for several moments. Anippe studied the boat. Where were the guards?

As though reading her mind, the old man spoke again, his tone different, a reverence encircled the words. "Do not fear the guards, child. They are gone. For the rising of many moons and many suns, we have moored thus, the tongueless guards gone to their families, leaving only the silent and blind slaves locked in the hatch and two guards. By now, they all sleep. I am old. No one has tried to rescue me. They are all safe, they believe. Now, tell me, does the child exist? Is it a boy? Do not tell me more for fear my resolve might desert me."

"Yes, there is such a boy-child."

"Then the time has come for us to strike." The old man smacked one hand onto the other.

"How? How will this be done, Reverend Father?" she asked. "No one even knows where you are."

"But you do. You will tell them."

Anippe sat in silence again. She had come this far with no idea how to go further.

"There are those that sent you on this quest," he continued. "You only need to tell them and they will do the rest. Go, make known what you have found."

Her sides shook with a hollow laugh. "How am I going to tell anyone? How am I going to get out of here?"

"Over the side, and soon. Others will be returning to take up this sham for another day. You must go soon."

"I can not swim., I got here without thinking of what I was doing. I am afraid."

"You must go. I will pray for your safe passage, but go."

He did not hear her creep to the rail, or swing herself over, or even drop into the water, but felt her fear as it closed over her. "Save her," he prayed. "Save us all."

Though Anippe had entered on the shore side, the river caught her, bouncing her off the rough boards and swirling her away. Coughing and sputtering, she finally landed on a small sandbar. After pulling herself out of the muddy water, she wanted only to rest. Instead, she begged a ride in a donkey cart traveling up the winding dirt road back into the city.

CHAPTER 38

Awakening in the early dawn, a man praised the gods of his house. He had been granted another day in the light before he opened his eyes to the darkness. Laying still, he listened to the others of his extended family, the snoring, grunting, or movement that signaled they also were rousing. He lay still, waiting for the sound of the horns that rang throughout the city to mark the passage of time. While he lay still, he remembered the events of days past.

He thought of the metalworker who had gazed in awe at the ram's head talisman. Wiry with heavy scars on his arms and hands, the man had melted the piece into thin ribbons of gold before breaking them into flecks. He had taken his share, then turned from the guardsman as he departed. His brother, the rug weaver, had taken his share and was cautioned to hide it well and tell no one. So he had done so. The flecks that were left were hidden within the very walls of this house, above his sleeping head; only his wife knew where.

He could just see the vague silhouette of his wife nursing her newborn child. His hand ran across her face, feeling the heated place where vague discoloring still showed the bruises. The woman flinched at his touch. She would not again be party to anything so foolish that it might endanger his family, no matter the reward.

CHAPTER 39

Hakeem had cautioned about eyes that would see, tongues that would tell, and the dangers that abounded, especially for slaves perceived to have crossed the line of caste. Anippe had no tattoo that spoke of her ownership by the House of Pharaoh. To hide the missing mark, she wore a tattered cloth covering the area as though it were a pus-filled abomination. Thus far, none had challenged it, but her luck had run mostly to the immediate need Loust had for slaves to work within the palace. A city contained within itself, there were literally tens of thousands of occupants whose lives were not worth a second glance. Thousands died when Manu had overthrown his brother; new slaves had to be imported quickly. It would not do for any to be as raw captives here were because they might endanger the Royals. Rather, they should be siphoned off from the households of others. Only the smug contentment of Loust and the supporters of Manu, who believed they had nothing to fear, had allowed her to be overlooked.

When she'd arrived back at the palace, dirty and exhausted, she approached a smaller gate on the downriver side. Selecting an elderly guard, she had tearfully explained that she had fallen in the river at the Queen's Palace and been swept away.

"Oh, poor child. Who shall I summon?" Concern creased the man's weathered face.

"There are none, good father. Only allow me to return to my Queen and beg mercy."

Anippe had only a few options before her. Between them, in the brief seconds they spoke, Hakeem and Anippe had devised a list where he should look for her. The time had come when she needed to look for him. Today, even though she was clean of the river's stench, exhaustion permeated her bones. She knelt in the shade of the date and palm trees on her soothsayer's rug, not harking her abilities but fighting the need to curl up and sleep. Perhaps the triplets would come today.

"If you fall over, you will break your pretty nose."

Her head snapped up. Seated nearby as he fed the small birds was Hakeem. His eyes darted everywhere, looking for lurking dangers. When he spoke, his lips did not appear to move though she could hear, and cherish, his every word.

A woman knelt before Anippe. Rahaf wore a caftan of palest yellow and smelled of sandalwood and clean desert nights. From her robe, she extracted a small bundle which she laid beside her as she dropped her offering into Anippe bowl.

Anippe cast her bone dice. "I have found Omari," Anippe said.

A grunt was her only reply.

"I have spoken to him. He told me to tell others it is time."

Hakeem's eyes, dark and hard, met hers, then turned away. A frown skewered his smooth features.

"He is on a river barge. He has been there for a long time. Daily the Queen questions him."

"We have heard this tale," snorted Hakeem.

"The barge bears a flag of gold on green with two black marks from the bottom left to upper right. The barge also bears those colors."

"There is a wine merchant whose fleet shows that flag," said Rahaf.

Giggling concubines passed. Both women leaned closer to the dice.

"They are supposed to row day and night, but it is not so. At sunset the barge is far from the city and they anchor. Everyone leaves. The slaves are locked in the hull and only two guards remain with the old man."

Again, the questioning grunt.

Anippe's spine stiffened. "I was on the barge,"

The others shifted.

"I was hidden. But, when darkness was deep, and all was quiet, I spoke with Omari, for it is only then that he is allowed above decks."

"Where is this place they stop for the night?"

"I do not know. Below here. When I went back into the river, the current dragged me through many reeds before I finally landed on a sandbar and was able to pull myself from the water." Anippe could feel the concern from the others. "I begged a ride in a donkey cart, saying I was from the palace and had fallen in the river. We did not arrive at the city until mid-afternoon and we were on the other side of the river. I did not see where the soldiers or oarsmen went when they left the barge, but there must have been a village nearby because they were back at first light."

"Is that all?" Hakeem asked.

Had she failed him? Did he need more? Anippe bit her lip, thinking.

No, she thought, shaking her head. She had nothing else.

Rahaf rose, moving sedately away. The bundle remained. Anippe drew it to her.

"In the King's Palace is a slave corridor that leads to the aqueducts. Do you know it?" asked Hakeem.

Ankh nodded.

"I will wait for you there." He said, tossing a few coins down.

"How will you remain unseen?" Anippe asked. When no answer came, she raised her head. The bench was empty, the birds scattered on the wind.

CHAPTER 40

The bundle, packed before she had reentered the city, contained attire different from what Anippe had worn previously. Alone, she rolled the bundle open and found a small, tight-fitting halter awash with embroidery and glittering stones. The fabric was a rich dark purple. The same fabric made the v-shaped girdle of harem pants of the sheerest gauze. These also were heavily decorated and included a large teardrop pearl on the front. The inner short pants which ended at her thigh were purple silk, but the voluminous sheer legs were white, vaguely tinted to lavender and ended at a tight cuff on her ankle. There were rings for her toes, armlets, and another wig. This one, more ornate, had another pearl which hung in the middle of her forehead, the sister to the one on the girdle.

After washing in a deserted fountain, Anippe traced her eyes with charcoal, accenting their color and shape before donning the outfit. She had lost weight and the deep V in the girdle, which should have lain just below her bellybutton, now fitted slightly lower. There was a short, diaphanous veil that covered her face below her eyes. This outfit, more Arabian than Egyptian, was meant to draw notice to her. The time for hiding in the shadows was done.

No fear coursed through Anippe's veins now, though it had when she had packed the bundle. She did not touch the beads below the pearl, but merely verified they were still there. After attaching the veil, she turned to face the Palace of Pharaoh, the den of all thieves and the greatest murder of her time.

CHAPTER 41

Each building had its own Domo, who was provided with an opulent apartment within that building's walls. In the Queen's Palace, it was no different. Rarely seen by outsiders due to the pilfered wealth secreted within, Domo Sidet held interviews in an enclosed courtyard for those who brought information regarding the hidden sects that abounded within the great Egyptian empire. He made no secret of his bribery, encouraging one man to turn on his neighbor. A slave's reward might be a slightly raised status, an easier place, or a woman to share his mat. A free man's reward was more financial.

The guard had spent the hours since waking trying to conjure a way to explain the small golden flecks gouged from the ram's head so he could use them. Standing with his men outside the harem doors, overseeing traffic in the great corridor, an idea had presented itself.

"So, you saw a slave..."

Sidet paced before the man, kneeling with his head bowed. Each step was accented by the heavy beat of Sidet's staff against the marble flagging.

The man spoke again, slower, trying to organize his rambling. "Several months ago, I noticed a female slave. I saw her many places, vaguely attending to nothing. I thought she was perhaps avoiding her responsibilities. Unfortunately, my duties stopped me from being able to question her."

"Why did you notice her to begin with?"

"She had...a way about her that did not match her rank. Her manner was secretive yet prideful, though she should not be. There was something in the way she walked, the way she looked about her as if she carried power and right. Many times, I witnessed her talking to others who worked steadily while she patted the air. When they were questioned, they admitted not knowing who she was, but said she was very inquisitive."

"She talked to other slaves?" Sidet's impatience was beginning to shine through his veneer.

"Yes, I saw her in the kitchens, at the barge docking,

and then she started telling fortunes. Many days, I saw her with the other seers, speaking to the underlings of Queen Kanika.

Sidet stood in front of the man, staff raised. He was bored and not pleased to have his time wasted. "Is that all?"

"No," said the man, still bowed, but aware of being beneath the staff. "There is a whisper that the asp found in the Queen's bath was released by this woman."

"Where did this whisper come from?" Sidet's eyes narrowed, the staff lowered.

Now a trembling filtered through the man's bowels, for here he must show the most stealth. "When I was going to my home late one evening after the horns of Ra had announced the sunset, I followed a crowd of men who laughed and spoke of a trick played on the Queen. One of the men hissed like a snake. When I interrupted them, asking of what they spoke, they ran away. I was only able to catch one, barely more than a boy. He told me he did not know the others, but was merely listening as was I. Then after the incident, I was told one of the slaves who was cleaning had found a small sack near where the snake had been found. The slave remarked of a woman who had been not previously in the baths who was there on this day and that she carried such a sack." Even to his own ears, this tale sounded false.

"You have no other witnesses? No other knowledge?"

"No, master."

"Would you know this woman?"

"Yes," answered the guard. The breath escaping his chest caused him great pain.

Sidet stood, tapping his foot nervously. Finally, he threw four clay coins down in front of the man. He had seen the dead asp and been told of this found sack. It gave the story credibility. He allowed the man to leave, knowing he could be easily found later.

CHAPTER 42

One day had passed. Anippe had walked the corridors of

Pharaoh's Palace, carefully following a man each time who

could be assumed to be her master. Pharaoh had not walked the

corridor, and it was he she sought. If he did not see her, find

her, be drawn to her , she would need to brave the lion in the

audience chamber. That was not a place where one could

wander in.

    She paused, looking for another unknowing escort. A

shadow passed overhead, and a chill slid along her arms.

Anippe turned her gaze upward, but nothing showed in the hot

blue sky, bleached by the sun, to a thin transparent blue.

Shivering with dread, Anippe plucked a thread from her

jeweled girdle. Casting the tiny piece of cotton from her, she

ducked her head while asking Ra to remove the evil that had

just crossed her path. Hopefully, this small superstition would protect her.

Far down the corridor, a horn blew. Everyone in the courtyard, including Anippe, turned. Pharaoh was seated, ready for the day. She did not see the thread, caught on an errant wisp of wind, turn back to land hidden in the folds of her glittering gauze trousers—a bad omen.

That day she had been here for less than two clicks of the sundial. There was a heavy commotion behind her, but she did not turn. The man she followed had an entourage of seven or eight and two carried numerous scrolls. Hopefully, they would pass the guarded entrance and she would be drawn in their wake.

CHAPTER 43

Gorge rose in the throat of the guard as he faced one of Sidet's minions, a spindly legged youth who ordered the guard to follow him. The guard had hoped for a few coins that would fill his family's bellies, perhaps allow for a new mat or length of cloth, but not so much that he'd be drawn further into the political web that lived here, fanged and hungry.

His fear deepened when Sidet, who had spent a long and sleepless night, stated that together they would go to Loust. There, Sidet added, the guard would again tell his story. So they had marched through the corridors and across the pavilions. The sun was hot but not the cause of the sweat that ran down the man in rivulets. Sidet's men encircled him, perhaps innocently, but effectively holding him in place.

When they arrived in the area Anippe haunted, they were met by Sidet's runner, sent ahead to alert Loust that Sidet would need time with his overlord. Sidet loudly summoned the runner again, proclaiming his need. People turned at the sound of his shrill order. A pathway opened before them. The guard gasped. There she was, several steps ahead of him. She walked without looking back. He would know that gait anywhere. Many times he had noticed her, watched her walk pastwith her innocent allure and lithe frame, wondering which lucky man was assigned to this wench.

He grabbed Sidet's arm. Sidet turned abruptly, shocked a slave would touch him.

"There, Master. There is the woman," the guard said.

Sidet forgot the inappropriate sweating palm against his forearm. He, too, looked ahead. There were many, including an Arabic contingent, moving away.

"Where?" Sidet asked.

The guard had already released his grip and was moving past, his movement so abrupt even those who surrounded him leaped back in surprise. Six long steps and he was upon her, shouting "Stop, woman!"

Anippe turned when some of the women she followed

turned. There had been a small commotion behind her, but it was not unusual here and she had greater business. The guard's face was within inches of her own, his hands already grasping her. Leaning back to pull away, Anippe encountered the hard frame of Sidet's personal guard while still another closed in on her other side. Anyone she could have claimed to be with moved discretely out of range. Her instinct was to fight; her mind whispered prudence.

"This is the woman," the guard announced to Sidet as the Domo approached. "The woman with the asp."

"Asp!" Anippe gasped, leaning closer to one of the burly men as for protection, her eyes darting about the area in fear.

"Be quiet!" Sidet ordered, stepping between them, efficiently separating the man from the woman. He looked at her for a long time as she stood with downcast eyes. She did not look familiar to him. Sidet believed that if she had been in the Queen's Palace for a long period of time, he would recognize her. What a beauty she was. Though Sidet was a eunuch and had no need of a woman, he knew others who would pay a healthy purse for one such as this. His own "wife" who saw to his personal affairs and companioned him was not this lovely.

A frown crossed his brow. Loust would expect him to appear soon. Sidet had sent word he was coming to assure time with his liege. Even if he did not take the woman with him, the foolish guard would probably speak of it. Sighing deeply, Sidet prayed silently for Loust to overlook the woman.

A boy messenger appeared at Sidet's elbow. "Master," he said, crumbling to the floor. "Master, Loust awaits."

There was no time to interview her, no time to think of a different plan. Sidet turned on his heel, following the messenger. "Bring them both," he commanded.

It was disparaging for Sidet to have the messenger turn away from the direction of Loust's office and enter the throne room. Once inside the great doors, the boy turned aside, no longer following the pathway to Pharaoh, Exalted, and Great within the Eyes of The Gods.

A corridor ran around the outside of the enormous room, contained by columns on the inside and a wall of doors on the other. Prior to this time, the wall had been latticed and led to large meeting rooms. Now the walls were more substantial, a place hidden from prying eyes for secret meetings and disreputable negotiations.

The boy, known to the clerk in attendance just inside the main door, was waved through without preamble. Anippe was ushered through with the group. She was not restrained, simply surrounded tightly by guards. The man that had reported her was similarly occupied and walked ahead of her. She could just see the top of his shining head and wondered how he knew her. As they moved deeper into the room where opulent treasures as well as a huge number of muscular men, each in a short white skirt, with heavily oiled skin, and carrying large deadly looking spears, were gathered, Anippe's thoughts ran only to fear. She said goodbye to her son and Hakeem and forced herself to stand tall as she marched along.

Loust stood at a stone table surrounded by his scribes and aides. Many clay tablets were stacked before him. They listed the day's petitioners, their status, requests, tributes, and bribes. The messenger was replaced by an aide, who stood in attendance until Loust could grant a moment of time.

Sidet bowed before the man who stoked flames of fear in bellies of many. Tersely, Sidet explained the situation and offered the guard as proof. Behind them, Anippe waited. If she would die here, she would not cower. She stood with her head up, tense but not fearful. Her guards had moved slightly away from her, leaving a small open space around her.

A shaft of bright sunlight speared through an opening in the roof. Pharaoh, bored with the whining lament of the merchant before him, looked for Loust to remove the man. Instead, he saw the woman encased in light.

The juices of his loins ran. Waving his hand in dismissal, he called out to Loust.

CHAPTER 44

An aide pulled the still speaking petitioner from the room while Loust waved Pharaoh's followers away. Though there appeared to be few in the cavernous hall, close to sixty who normally attended Pharaoh, hung about. Priests, seers, aides, physicians, councilors, and selected others comprised the daily train that accompanied Pharaoh. Due, however, to his corrupt dealings with the petitioners, Pharaoh allowed only one petitioner to enter at a time. This was a great difference from his brother, who had filled the hall daily. There were even stone benches behind the columns for the multitude to sit beyond the view of Pharaoh. Now they stood empty, gathering dust.

Also in attendance were those who followed the Queen, currently seated beside Pharaoh. Her followers stood in the outer circle beyond those attended who Pharaoh. In the area beyond Loust's worktable, Sidet positioned himself so that, should she look, Kanika would not spot him. He was sure things would end badly for him if she found this interruption was his fault.

Loust approached Pharaoh, kneeling before him and speaking in hushed tones. All the while, Pharaoh's eyes were on the woman. On Pharaoh's left, Queen Kanika belatedly noticed a change in the atmosphere.

"What is it?" she asked.

Manu, Pharaoh of Egypt, Prince of the Nile, Lord of the Sun and All Its Minions, waved his hand, silencing her. She leaned closer. Loust, who feared no one in the room save Pharaoh, pressed his lips together. Even the parasite that was Pharaoh's Queen did not instill fear within him. He waited for his lord to speak.

"Hm," said Pharaoh, "I tire of the ramblings of penury men. It will amuse me to listen to this slave speak. She is a slave, is she not?"

"Yes," Loust said, "though we know not whose yet." Loust approached Anippe, instructing her to approach the bottom step but not advance from there. "You will kneel silently until Pharaoh speaks, then answer clearly. Do not raise your eyes to his glory, for death will follow swiftly."

Anippe prostrated herself on the marble floor before Pharaoh.

"I have heard of you. You are a seer, a...witch!"

"No, Great One, I am not a witch. Those who have told you these things have perhaps..." She paused, her face darkened.

"Have what? Are you to tell me that my faithful people have lied?" he bellowed. Others surrounding him shrank back.

Anippe's voice remained low and calm. This was not the time to challenge Pharaoh. "Most Exalted of all, I fear that others have a higher regard for my abilities than any power I could obtain. I am merely a grain of sand in the great desert that is the strength of Pharaoh." Gracefully, she rose slightly, advancing to the first step, her arms extended towards the dais, palms raised in supplication.

Above her, the fat man relaxed among his cushions. She was akin to his penned gazelles; brazen, nervous creatures vaulting the fences with ease but never allowing a touch. The melody of her voice lingered in his mind, as did the image of her smooth, unblemished skin. Saliva filled his mouth, bubbling lightly in the corner of his lips as he grinned. "Today you will sit here, to my right. When I am through with the others who demand my notice, we will speak again."

The Queen snorted her displeasure but said not a word. She wanted the girl sent away; punished, not revered. Loust, always aware of Pharaoh's predilections, returned to his work.

Anippe perched on the hard-stone bench to the right of the dais, the intricate carvings unnoticed as she listened to the business of Pharaoh. Perhaps among the chaff she would find a few kernels to be used when the time was right.

In only a short time, Pharaoh cajoled his Queen to be about her own business. She was obstinate and would not leave.

Anippe felt Manu's gaze on her often. She trembled slightly. It was too late to question the safety of her position. Peering through her lashes, she noted his heightened color and his leering gaze that did not care who noticed. Soon the sun would rise to its most glaring height. Pharaoh tried one more time to send his Queen on her way gracefully.

"No, my beloved," she replied, "my only appointment for this day is to remain at your side, basking in your love and returning my own to you."

Everyone seated within hearing range stopped and stared. The Queen's bad temper and biting tongue were legendary. Though she and her husband often baited each other, she rarely used this honeyed sarcasm against him. It was her way of using this caressing tone only to those who would soon forfeit their lives for one minor offense or another.

Pharaoh grunted in response. He had moved as close to where Anippe sat as his huge throne allowed. Now he moved back to the center and sat crossing the Royal staffs across his chest. Only his Queen and Anippe heard his next words. "Go. Go now and keep your evil mouth shut."

The Queen leaned back from his wrath, her mouth open to retort.

"Hear I but one sound from you and your stable of young boys will be gutted on the very bed you share with them."

Rising shakily, the Queen continued to stare at him. Never before had Pharaoh spoken to her in such terms. Their perversions were more often a shared pastime. Her great weight shivered in response, but with head held high, she swished from her seat and ignoring the small exit door to the side of the throne, walking regally down the center aisle. Her entourage fell in quickly behind her. Just beyond the door, her legs gave way. It took five burly men to heft her into the ornate sedan chair that waited.

Anippe's mouth was dry. It was harder to smile now.

When the last of the Queen's entourage had left the throne room, Pharaoh signaled Loust. "We are done today."

He did not rise until Loust had emptied the room. It took two guards to assist him as he pulled his bulk upright. Anippe was repulsed, but sat still. "Come," Pharaoh said with a smile as he left the dais. "We will eat and know each other better."

The glint in his eye shouted a warning, but though she hesitated, Anippe chose to ignore. The time for retreat had passed.

Though it had been a long while since last she walked the Pharaoh's Palace halls, she knew he would dine in his private quarters, which followed a long walk through many halls and up many stairs. She knew not to walk with Pharaoh but to blend in with those who followed.

Manu did not leave the council chamber. Instead, he walked to a place where a large resplendent Persian carpet hung on the wall. Guards sprang forth, pulling open a wide door on which the carpet was attached. Inside, Anippe saw a large, opulent room, Pharaoh's new private quarters. Slaves waved large feathered fans and filled the low tables with food. There was seating here for several.

Pharaoh lowered himself to a wide couch strewn with pillows. His manservant removed his master's headpiece; Pharaoh's naked head was drenched with sweat. Brass and gold jewelry were peeled off, much of it hiding in folds of fat, until only the rings too small for his great fingers remained. Anippe stood quietly while Pharaoh was made comfortable.

"Sit here, child. Near me." Two slaves knelt between

the table and Pharaoh's couch. "We will eat. I am sure you are as hungry as I. We will be as friends." Almost immediately, the slaves started stuffing his great maw.

Once seated, Anippe realized that, other than the clerk and slaves, only she had accompanied Pharaoh here. They ate in silence. Whole fowls were denuded of their meat, disappearing into the cavernous gullet. Fruit which had already been peeled and sliced was followed by wine, sweetmeats, and food Anippe could not even identify. Sated by a few slices of melon and a single thin slice of roasted dove, she watched the feeding of her ruler with rising disgust. Whole villages did not see this much food in a day.

When she could stand it no more, the great mound of humanity belched loudly, causing Anippe's bile to rise. Fighting her own repulsion, she spoke softly. "I did not remember this room being here."

"Huh?' Pharaoh gulped down the last mouthful, belching repeatedly. It was obvious he was not normally interrupted while he ate. "Remember?"

"In my mind's eye, I have often envisioned the glory of

your realm." A bead of sweat ran down Anippe's back.

"Oh, yes, because you are a seer, you would know much." He waved the slaves away. Grease shone on his face. Wiping it away with his hand, he peered at Anippe expectantly. She sat quietly. He continued, "You are right not to envision this place. Before it was a few small rooms where private councils were held, but I could not see why I, Pharaoh, would want to be so far from the center of my power, so I had that altered. It took many hours to create this room and to carve the hidden doorway. Quite clever, do you not think?"

"Yes, very clever." She stood and moved around the seating area, studying the treasures displayed. Clasping her hands together to hide her trembling, she made herself ready to do what must be done, but wanting it over with. For a long while, she had worked to this end. She had even vowed to die in the effort, but what about Gadi? If she succeeded, her son, the next Pharaoh, would be well taken care of and the murderer of thousands would be dead. She also knew that, when Gadi became Pharaoh, she would no longer exist in his world. She, his mother, would be unknown. It was a sacrifice she was willing to make and was steadier now than before. The power in her head spoke loudly.

In her heart, a small voice repeated, "What about Hakeem?" This was not where she was supposed to be. He would not find her here.

"Why do you wander, girl?" grunted her master from his couch. It was well that his slaves had divested him of all but a loincloth, for there were bits of food and smears of grease covering his face and torso. To look upon him revolted her. Anippe forced the taut muscles in her back to relax. Tossing back her head, she threw him an inviting smile.

"There are so many beautiful things here. I am over-awed by the wonders that surround you." She moved further away, swaying her hips as she went. The small bells embroidered into her girdle twinkled lightly.

"Come here, my sweet. Perhaps a pretty bauble will come your way."

She moved closer slowly, giggling in what she considered a girlish manner. Pharaoh obviously found it alluring, for his smile grew. He stretched out, beckoning her with his thick hands, each stubby finger encircled in gold. Fidgeting with the beads dangling from her waist, she hesitated, throwing a meaningful look towards the fanning slaves and guards, and then she dropped her eyes, feigning embarrassment by their presence.

"OUT!" he bellowed. "GET OUT!"

It was not until the last rushing guard left that Anippe moved again. She had been searched before she entered the Grand Chamber and had been found safe to leave with Pharaoh. Even his private guard hurried away. Hidden in her hand, she held the two bottom beads from the girdle of her harem pants. She could not hold them long, for they were very potent and the sweat on her palm would allow entry through her skin. Gracefully, she took up her half-full wine goblet, dropping the beads in, unseen, as she swung about.

"What if the Queen arrives, Master?" she asked demurely.

Pharaoh was panting. "She will not come in unannounced. No one will come in now until I ring for them." The summons bell was well within his reach. Once again, he motioned her nearer.

Slowly, she came around the table, moving the brass bell back as she put the goblet down. She was close enough that he could smell her perfume. Grasping the gauzy fabric of her trousers, he pulled her closer, snuffling her heady scent within the fabric. Now he held her hand. She smiled and fluttered her lashes against her cheeks as she pulled so slightly away. But he would have none of it. He pulled her down to the seat next to him, fumbling with her tight-fitting brocade halter.

"Tut, tut." She chided, pushing his hands away to unclasp the gold lion's head. He did not wait for her measured removal, but pushed against the offending garment. Sliding onto her knees, she allowed him to fondle her breasts, grasping and pinching until his eyes became slits among the rolls of fat. Leaning across him, her breasts caressing his face, she reached for the goblet. His eyes sprang open when she leaned back from him. Another coy smile, and she put the goblet to her lips moving her mouth as though to savor the taste, but she did not drink. In the manner of a docile woman making an offer to her lover, she put the vessel to his lips. Gulping down the remainder of the wine, he snatched the empty goblet from her and tossed it aside. The metal hit stone and rattled loudly, putting her teeth on edge.

"Enough with your virgin guile," he ordered. Grasping her trousers, he sought to remove them. If she was to escape, she would need her clothes intact. Her smile was forced, her lips rigid with a tension Pharaoh did not notice as she removed all until she stood naked before him. Sweat ran in small streams down his chest and bald head. She lifted the loin cloth, barely able to find his pathetic manhood between his fat, sloppy thighs.

Why does he still breathe? She wondered, worried that his great size would not succumb to the two tiny beads of poison.

"Now," he ordered.

She straddled him, unsure if his penis was long enough to reach within her. His hands still grasping her breast suddenly fell away. His mouth opened, and his vacant eyes stared at the ceiling.

Like a cat, she bound off him, vomiting as soon as she

hit the floor. Though she knew she had to hurry, she took up a napkin, rubbing her body clean of his touch before she slipped back into her clothes. Now to escape. The plans that she and Hakeem had devised would not work; she had only herself to rely on.

Anippe arranged Pharaoh, so it appeared he napped among his pillows, a foil to fool any curious interloper. Then she used the same square of cloth to clean her hands. She quickly moved around the room, looking for whatever escape she could find. It wasn't until she crept out on the balcony and looked down into the peacock's pen that she thought she might actually get away. The peacocks, though feisty, did not fly. The outside wall was low and their pen was liberally lined with straw. True, the corridor on the other side was for the gamekeeper, but perhaps she could exit there. Even as she considered this, she heard voices behind her call, "Master?"

She threw her legs over the stone railing and dropped among the birds, whose immediate screeching brought those above to the edge of the railing. The gamekeeper came running and pulled open the door. The man fell back in fear as the peahen Anippe had snatched up flew into his face.

Slipping past him, Anippe sprinted along the corridor. At that moment, his assistant entered the far side, unaware of what had occurred. Egged on by the cries of his master and Pharaoh's screaming servants, the young man took up the chase, leaping over the elderly gamekeeper. In front of Anippe was a split door, which provided an exit to the next alleyway. The bottom was closed, but she dove headfirst through the opening above, rolling to her feet on the other side. Behind her, she could hear the fumbling of a latch and running feet. The alley way was cluttered with bales, bags of feed, and carts of excrement. Small and lithe, Anippe darted from one open space to another, running or leaping over obstacles where her heavier pursuer could not. She was unable, however, to stop his screaming voice from alerting those ahead.

Barely escaping the grasping hands of those who would block her path, the young woman knew her time of freedom was drawing to an end. Ahead, another gateway showed. Should the door be slammed shut, she would be trapped with no hope of escape.

Behind her, the assistant shouted, "Close the gate!"

Suddenly the tail and back quarters of a camel appeared, a sight brown and beautiful. Moving backwards, the beast blocked the door, which was being pressed against his rear haunches. Sliding beneath the beast, Anippe rolled to safety. She did not fear the animal's hooves because she knew the camel would not step on her. The assistant did not appear to have the same faith and shuddered to a halt with his nose inches from the camel's furred ass.

Camels surrounded her. This alleyway, wider than the others, was filled with camels and confusion. Drivers yelled; whips flashed. The camels reacted to their riders and pressed among the people. All those on foot scurried out of reach, pushing their fellows out of the way. On either side, strong brown hands descended, grabbing Anippe by the upper arms and flinging her over the alley wall.

Airborne, arms and legs whirling freely, she pictured a mound of broken bones when she landed. A man standing in a rough cart caught her. A heavy amok was pulled over her and she was set stumbling on her feet among those who were fleeing the bedlam erupting from the Palace.

The great brass horns sounded the attack on the House of Pharaoh. Soon, the compound would be sealed and none would be able to leave. Armed guards would corral everyone, and many would suffer. Already, the great gates were closing. There would be no escape.

When she started to follow the mob headed down the gateway corridor, a hard pinch pulled her aside. Through the small, netted eye opening, she could see another amok, as common as hers.

"This way," said a voice. "They will be stacked at the gates like dung by the fire pit, screaming and fighting for escape."

They did not move alone. Several other persons, both male and female, all in similar Muslim attire, moved in the direction they did. This pathway led to a narrow-enclosed walkway headed towards the neighboring temple. The ornate metal gate was closed. When the horns had sounded, all the gates had been closed, locking the palace inhabitants and any others inside.

At the gate, an old man stepped forward from their party of eight. Words she could not understand were exchanged, coins she heard clink together, changing hands. The gate opened a crack. They all squeezed through before it slammed shut again, even as others approached. At a bend in the corridor, a stone moved in the wall and she was pushed inside a dark staircase. Her hand found a heavy rope rail. Prodded by those who went before her and those that followed, she descended.

The air was close. Breathing was difficult in the amok. Anippe tried to keep her footing. When she stumbled, her companions grabbed her robe. At the bottom, they moved in to another narrow corridor. Here a waiting slave, eyes averted, held a torch to light their way. It offered a small amount of welcomed light.

When they came to the end of their trek, they faced another wall of stone. Silently, her guides settled onto the floor and the torch died. Time passed slowly.

Anippe could stand it no longer.

"How did you find me?" She whispered, to the person

in the amok beside her.

An even lower whisper came back. "We have walked the hallways, corridors, and pathways of the palace for many days. We knew you were coming."

Finally, a section of the stone walls quietly slid aside. The opening was low to the ground. The men crawled through on their hands and knees. Even the women were too tall to walk out into the world. Their exit was hidden behind a basket-maker's stall. The man and his family were gone; night had settled over Egypt.

The group moved in single file. Staying close to the tall walls, they moved down winding streets. When the slap of feet or yelling voices erupted, they took on the appearance of the homeless beggars, huddled balls of rags, and humanity seeking refuge in a small group against naked stone.

Many small groups of soldiers searched for the assassin. Here, outside the walls of the Palace, beggars were common place and unseen. Any person who ran or looked about in fright might be guilty and was apprehended to be questioned. The gates opened only far enough to allow these poor souls to be dragged through and then were slammed shut again.

No words had been spoken, only grunts of command since Anippe's involuntary vault over the inner wall. She did not know who she followed, but she knew they could not escape the city; all gates closed at dusk. By dawn, the soldiers of Pharaoh would be searching for any who tried to leave.

This was a poorer section of the city. The ground underfoot was a rough combination of dirt and splintered paving. Even with the short steps the amok allowed her to take, Anippe tripped often, colliding with her companions. Following a winding path, they eventually came to a watering trough fed through a clay pipe from above. The constant trickle of water kept the trough reasonably full. The ground surrounding it was damp, though firm. During the day, when women filled water jugs and animals quenched their thirst, the mud was nearly ankle deep.

"Rest," said a man, motioning for them to sit.

The two women, and Anippe pulled off their amoks. A single piece robe of lightweight fabric, was pulled over

Anippe's head. "Remove your garments," instructed one of the women.

Under the robe, Anippe removed the ornate bodice and harem pants she had donned at the palace. She had long ago lost her wig. One of her companions handed her a heavier robe of coarsely woven wool. Now they were all dressed in loose, dark robes, silent shadows in the moonless night. A large hood hung from the back and she pulled it over her head. The tall man collected her clothing, and the discarded amoks, balling them together and stuffing the bundle in the mud behind the fountain. Eventually, someone would find it, but they would be gone.

On the far side of this small neighborhood, was a wooden hatch against the outside wall. It ran from the height of a man's knees to his shoulder. This hatch was used by those who daily collected the human excrement to cast it out of the city into the river that ran behind the wall. No one used this hatchway without paying a tithe. Tonight, no tithe collector sat on the mud bench, playing guard and accountant. The wooden cover creaked in the dark. Anippe heard a call, someone answered. One man went through the filthy opening, a woman followed. Anippe hesitated when her hands encountered the soft and reeking offal that lined the opening. Arms gathered her up and she, too, passed through the portal before the hatch closed.

Outside, where the Nile flowed against the wall, a small reed boat held her companions, the three who had just passed through the wall and a single oarsman. When all were seated, the men rowed together. There was no creaking of the oars against the boat. Far to her left, Anippe could see the Palace dock area. Hundreds of torches burned. The sound of metal clashing and men screaming was clear now, though within the city she had not heard it. Several barges were waiting at the water's edge, including those that looked like royal barges.

Anchored down river of the melee was a barge with green, white, and black striping—the prison of Omari, the displaced High Priest of Pharaoh's brother, he who had been the true Pharaoh. Omari, who would teach and guide Gadi. As she watched, a banner of gold on white rose, fluttered open to displace the banner of Queen Kanika. It was lit from below by lantern light. Other smaller crafts, bristling with armed men, encircled the barge and all moved toward the docking area. Around Anippe, the air seemed to crackle and snap with energy. Anippe cowered. Though she had known death would be the result of her actions, she had not considered the cost of a battle.

On the far shore, she was helped from the boat, then fell into step between the man and the woman. This section of the city housed those persons of no influence, the crowded tenements of the freemen. Here narrow and crooked streets were lined with running gutters of waste. Scores of people rushed toward the water side. Men hid their wives behind them and some carried squalling children wrapped in ragged pieces of blanket. Their voices were not hushed but demanded of each other what news was available. The rumors Anippe heard were already great exaggerations of the truth.

Walking up the hill away from the water was exhausting. Not because of the climb, but the push against the wave of humanity that moved in the opposite direction. Anippe and the woman became separated from the man. The woman took her hand, pulling her closer as they fought further uphill. The tenements covered a large area and were very congested. It took several minutes to pass through the greatest throng to a place where fewer people stood, mostly women, ordered to stay behind by their men. The cries of children were louder and fear was a taste heavy in the air.

Anippe and the woman hesitated for only a moment. Their male companion struggled out of the crowd, rushing toward them. He drew them along only a short distance to an open place, a small courtyard filled with a broken fountain and a donkey cart. The driver was an emaciated man whose many years weighed his crippled form down. Tatters of black on high poles warned others to stay away. This was the cart of death, the cart of lepers, used to remove the diseased from the city. It did not matter the disease, Pharaoh ordered them gone.

Her escort pointed to the cart.

"No," Anippe said, trying to move away. The woman pushed her back, slapping and shoving until Anippe, shivering in fear, relented. With her robe wrapped tightly around her and her knees drawn to her chin, she sat upright in the middle of the cart, afraid to touch the wooden rails. Tears ran freely. Death hovered, waiting to be sucked into her lungs, to take her soul and claim it for his own beloved.

* * *

Bright sunlight woke Anippe. She had expected to be seated in the bottom of a gray and splintered boat, manned by a skeletal oarsman deep in the dark caverns that surrounded the River of Death. Anippe took a deep breath of relief. Standing, she held the rail against the rocking of the cart. In the distance, she could see the receding walls of the city. Great plumes of smoke billowed above it. Tiny specks of humanity fled the city. She watched in solemn silence, no longer frightened or angry or even curious. Anippe knew her life before this moment was gone, that Gadi was lost to her forever and, though her heart ached, she accepted this fate.

To the right, a flash caught her eye. She turned to see a horse, whose long, thick tail swished in impatience, standing on a dune. The rider was a man. He raised his arm before the horse pivoted and they disappeared over the sand. Anippe turned to the driver, but no words emerged from her dry lips.

Ahead were camels, standing placidly on the hot sand. A few men dismounted while their beasts chewed cud or napped, bored with the wait.

As the cart pulled alongside, the camels fell into step. On the lead camel, the rider removed his head wrappings, slowly unwrapping the yards of gauzy fabric as the animal neared where she stood. Anippe was entranced as she watched the actions of this desert wanderer. With a last tug, he was revealed. Hakeem smiled down, white teeth aglow in his dark face. Reaching in an exaggerated casual manner, his hand grasped hers and he pulled her up into the saddle with him.

"Ah," he said, "my desert Princess."

Other Books by this Author

Strength of the Mayan Leopard

Wu Lee

Murder in the Meadow

Diary of a Mad Woman

Willa the Wisp

Made in United States
North Haven, CT
26 August 2025

72164243R00212